ALIEN ATTRACTION

"On my world, such a request by a stranger would be met with death."

"We're not on your world," said Hughes, "and it's interesting that you express such violence."

"You will follow?"

"I can stand at the door," said Hughes, "but I must keep you in sight."

She looked beyond him, to Brackett, as if appealing to a higher authority. Brackett said nothing. She waited and when she decided that she was going to get no help from him, she shrugged. She opened her robe and let it fall to her feet.

Brackett was surprised that she looked so human . . .

STAR PRECINCT

KEVIN RANDLE
AND
RICHARD DRISCOLL

ACE BOOKS, NEW YORK

STAR PRECINCT

An Ace Book / published by arrangement with
the authors

PRINTING HISTORY
Ace edition / April 1992

ISBN: 0-441-78268-X

Ace Books are published by The Berkley Publishing Group,
200 Madison Avenue, New York, New York 10016.
The name "ACE" and the "A" logo
are trademarks belonging to Charter Communications, Inc.

Prologue | A Simple Misunderstanding

The simulacrum, one of the new Bodyguard 4000 series, went berserk at 3:14 P.M. on the ninety-sixth floor of the Star Rest Imperium Hotel. The victim, later tentatively identified as Rama Lu O'Shaughnessy, a red-robed disciple of the Hare O'Shaughnessy splinter sect of the Hare O'Hara group, was stepping off the elevator when the Bodyguard deserted its post, rushed across the lobby, and grabbed the startled religious fanatic.

The Bodyguard, which could have been confused with a black-hatted villain in a Terran Wild West video, tore Rama Lu's right arm from the socket and then beat the religious zealot with it. Then, picking O'Shaughnessy up and holding him under its left arm, the robot slipped back to the elevator doors. It sent the car soaring toward the penthouse sixty stories above and finally pitched Rama Lu into the black void.

As O'Shaughnessy disappeared into the darkness, screaming all the way, the Bodyguard pivoted and returned to its post. The eight eyewitnesses, each fearing that one of them would be the next, scrambled to get the hell out of the way. But the Bodyguard, having completed its task, was no longer interested in any of the other living beings.

An hour later, the eyewitnesses sat in a special executive dining room that the Star Rest made available to only the richest and most important of its guests. The staff doctor had tranked those who had needed it, and now they all sat quietly, listening to the public relations director, a young blond woman who was using every weapon in her arsenal to keep the eyewitnesses happy.

The police arrived and were escorted into the dining room. They spread out among the witnesses, trying to determine what happened and why. They were interrupted thirty minutes later by the private secretary for the man who owned nearly everything on the planet's surface.

The police officer in charge whirled, stabbed a finger at the PR lady, and accused, "You didn't tell me Dennis Profitt was in residence today."

"I thought you knew."

The private secretary, a woman with a slightly reptilian look, watched the exchange and then said, "Mr. Profitt has a request."

"Anything," said the police officer and the PR woman together, sounding as if they had rehearsed the lines. "Anything."

"Mr. Profitt requests that you appeal to the Interplanetary Police for assistance."

"Shit," said the police officer.

"Star Cops," said the PR lady.

"Exactly," said the secretary before she turned to leave.

The PR woman looked at the police officer and said, "Now maybe we'll find out what's going on."

"Bullshit," said the cop, staring up, as if to seek guidance. "Bullshit."

1 | Some Enchanted Evening

No one could blame them for trying.

Not when the news videos inundated them with stories of former cops who gave up the badge for the word processor. Success by one tended to create an atmosphere where a lot of other cops were trying to cash in the same way.

"Now you can be just as famous as Lieutenant Dick Tracer who's making millions a year publishing the true tales of his personal adventures," ran one of the adverts in the *Badge*, a Star Precinct vidjournal.

Right now, as Lieutenant Richard Brackett walked down the halls of station number 107, which had been launched eighty-two years earlier, he saw just how many of his cops had believed the advert and were working on novels and vidplays.

Half the terminals on half the goddamned ship were tied up that way, which did not come as good news to a man whose idea of a fun evening was chasing a bad guy down a dark alley, then messing him up a little as he resisted arrest before beaming him around the system a few times before sending him to slumberland until the jailers woke him to begin the processing.

Brackett, who'd been on the force for eighteen years, hadn't always been that way. In fact, there had been a brief time when he'd been on the other side, indulging his desire for the good life by finding creative ways of removing the wealth from those who had more than their fair share. He had enjoyed the game, the hunt, as much as the final payoff. It was the use of his brain that he liked. Find the weakness, find the game the sucker was willing to play, and string him along until he handed you the fruits of his hard labor.

Then, eight years ago, he'd hooked up with a man named Janos, who had a plan that would lead them to the real big money. But Janos had decided that half of the big score wasn't enough. He wanted it all. To get it, he kidnapped Brackett's wife who was six months pregnant. Janos had hoped to lure Brackett in, take all the cash, and get out, but he couldn't keep his hands off Stephanie. He raped her and then killed her and had gotten out with the majority of the loot.

It took Brackett four weeks of relentless days and sleepless nights to find Janos, but find him he did. He trapped him in a shabby hotel room in the slums of Vesta. He gave Janos a chance. A slim one. Brackett took his own weapon and tossed it out the window, wanting to feel Janos die in his hands.

Janos recognized an advantage when he had one. And Janos was not as brave. He kept his own weapon and opened fire.

But madness had given Brackett a stealth he'd never had, and a desire he'd never known. Janos twisted the setting on his weapon to kill and then accidentally set the whole room on fire, but that did nothing to slow Brackett. He just kept moving, circling, advancing, and retreating.

Finally, standing there in the smoke-choked room, flames nearly covering the floor and hiding the walls, Brackett killed him. Beat him with his fists. Hammered at his head until Janos could no longer cry for mercy or help. Pounded on him until he was bleeding from the eyes, nose, mouth, and ears. And then punched him in the stomach until he began to vomit. He died, strangling on his own vomit.

Brackett had stood for a moment, looking at Janos's body, and then realized that his own clothing was beginning to smolder. He dove through the window, the fragile glass shattering. He ran down the rickety fire escape, leaving Janos to fry in the flames, which was good practice, considering the place Janos would spend eternity.

But the new Brackett was not the same as the old Brackett. A man can't pass through grief like that without being changed radically. Not if he's a man with a heart and a soul.

And he realized something else. His crusade against Janos was a crusade to bring the man to justice. No longer did he wish to separate the wealthy from their money. He wanted to see that what had happened to him didn't happen again.

He found himself entering the police academy. He passed the background check because he'd been clever enough to avoid the police during his swindling days, and because no one knew that he'd killed Janos. Of course, no one looked too hard when they found the burnt body.

Sometimes Brackett missed his old self. But not very often. Not anymore. He'd trained himself to tolerate, if not exactly like, what he'd become. And the search for the criminals allowed him to use his wit just as he had when working to con the wealthy.

At age forty-two, he had decided that it was about all he could expect from life.

As he completed his rounds, he heard a female voice say, "You think you can scare me just because you have a beamer? Well, you're wrong! Before I'll let you put one of your purple paws on me, I'll take this suicide pill I carry with me at all times. Do you understand me, infidel?"

Under most circumstances, Brackett would have leapt into action. Here was a woman in jeopardy, almost calling out for help. Or what sounded like it.

But Brackett saw the woman was seated at a small table near a viewport that opened onto the field of stars that surrounded the 107th. The woman was a very pretty redhead who was reading lines from a sheet of white paper. Sergeant Jennifer Daily was the precinct's resident expert on sociology and psychology. Unfortunately, she'd seen the same adverts as the others and was now trying to cash in.

"What do you think, Obo? Sound a little too melodramatic?" asked Daily.

"No, Sergeant Jennifer. It sounds very good. Very real. Very scared."

Obo was not human. He was humanoid. He stood over seven feet tall and weighed more than three hundred kilos in the precinct's artificial gravity. In the harsh lights of the station, irregularities in the peach fuzz that covered his body could be seen. In Earth normal sunlight, the peach fuzz would take on a slightly green tint that gave rise to many jokes about green men from Mars.

"Is very good," said Obo, using the peculiar phrasing that was common to the beings from Tau Ceti.

"God, Obo," said Daily, sounding like a breathless schoolgirl who'd just been asked to the prom, "you always make me feel great. Thanks."

She shuffled the papers together, glanced out the port, and then looked up to see Brackett standing there, scowling. Flushing as if she'd just been caught wasting valuable time, she said, "Hi, Loot. I was just reading Obo the end of chapter three. Want to hear it?"

"Right," said Brackett. "Right." And with that he walked off, leaving them behind him.

Brackett reached the stern of the precinct and stopped near the viewport in the Cup and Hole for a moment. It gave him a wide view of space near the precinct ship. Just gave a complete space as far as he could see. Bright points of light in every color burning through the black velvet of space.

Brackett shook himself and turned away from the viewport, thinking that he would soon be sitting in front of his word processor creating stilted prose for the potboilers and the vidscreens.

"Coffee, Loot?"

He turned and saw Wally Tate, a young man fresh from the ivory-towered world of college where he had studied the techniques of video journalism. He was a tall, skinny kid with light hair and no eyebrows, and the ability to stumble into, or trip over, everything. Brackett had decided that he was a good kid who had just a little too much enthusiasm for his own good.

"Yeah, give me a cup."

Tate stuck a cup under the spigot of the coffee maker and watched as the steaming liquid came out. It shut off automatically when the cup was full. He handed the Styrofoam cup to Brackett.

Brackett sipped from the cup trying to keep from burning his mouth. "Thanks," he said.

"No problem. Oh, Captain Carnes was looking for you a moment ago. Have you seen him?"

"No," said Brackett. And he didn't want to. Carnes was one of the "administrative" Star Cops who'd come up through the ranks by staying in the precinct shuffling papers and being pulled toward the top by family connections and highly placed family friends.

"He seemed to be upset about something," said Tate. He sipped his coffee, burned his tongue, and nearly choked while trying to look cool.

Brackett fought to keep a straight face. He turned his attention to the starfields outside the port. Lifting his cup to his lips, he took another drink.

"He wanted to see you right away, Loot," said Tate.

Brackett drained his cup, crushed it, and tossed it toward the recycler. It would break the cup down to its basic elements and reassemble them, along with other debris, into something else that would be useful. The one thing that life in space taught him was that you couldn't throw away anything.

"He's in his office," added Tate. "Told me to tell you that if I saw you."

"Always," said Brackett. He walked out of the coffee shop and made his way along the brightly lighted corridor. After eighty years in space, it was surprising how clean everything was. The tile of the deck looked to be as new as the day it was laid. There was no accumulated grime on the walls, or any of the hatches that led into the detective bays, the homicide area, the holding cells, the labs, or the administrative offices. There were areas on the deck that were worn, from four generations of feet, but it was still clean.

He reached the stern elevator, entered, and said, "Top level."

The elevator began to move. Brackett felt the movement in his feet and belly. He expected to head up, but the feeling was that he was falling. The doors opened and let Brackett out into the brightly lighted corridor of the upper level of the precinct. Here the deck was finely carpeted, the bulkheads were paneled in what looked to be dark woods from the shrunken rain forests of Earth.

Beyond there was always the distant rumble of the engines as the ship floated through space, but here, in the upper reaches of the precinct, that rumble was masked. It was as if the engines had been shut down.

Carnes had an office close to the elevator shaft. It showed that he was important, but not as important as the inspectors, the commanders, and the commissioners who administered and commanded the precinct.

Brackett stopped outside the hatch, ran his hands through his hair, and then laughed at himself. The actions had been automatic. Each time he was summoned to the upper levels, he made attempts to smooth his hair, to touch his face to determine if he needed to shave, and then glanced at his shoes to make sure they were shined.

But Brackett was meeting with Captain Carnes. Carnes didn't like him, hated him, in fact. Carnes knew of Brackett's unsavory background and didn't believe that a man like Brackett deserved to be a police officer.

Brackett reached out and touched the button next to Carnes's hatch. He looked up at the button camera mounted just over the center of the hatch and smiled broadly.

"Enter," said the voice from the speaker.

Brackett waved, wiggling his fingers at the camera, and stepped through the hatch as it irised open. Carnes's secretary sat behind a desk of metal and glass looking pert, competent, and willing. She was a slender blond woman in a short skirt and see-through blouse, and had she been a living being, Brackett would have asked her to have a drink with him in the Off Duty lounge where drinks, steaks, and members of the opposite sex congregated.

"You may enter the inner office," she said, sounding cold, professional, and slightly mechanical.

Brackett moved to the hatch, let it open, and then stepped through. It was almost like walking into another time in another place. The office was square, dark, and had a bank of windows that seemed to look out on a city at dusk. It was a holographic display that ran through the whole daylight cycle beginning when Carnes entered the office. It made it seem that an Earth normal day had passed.

Looking at the display, Brackett said, "Isn't it about time to knock off?"

Carnes, who was sitting behind a massive desk, looked up. He put his pen down, beside the green blotter that could have been used to refurbish a pool table. "It's my favorite time of day. Just enough light to see, but the city beginning to shine with neon and color." He turned in his chair and watched as more of the city's lights came on.

Without waiting to be asked, Brackett dropped into one of the large chairs set for visitors. Behind him was a couch shoved into a corner, along with a couple of chairs facing it creating a "conversation pit." It was a concept that had grown up in the twentieth century. Carnes had hung on to it.

Carnes finally turned away from the holo, opened a drawer, and pulled out a file folder. It was another anachronism. Most senior officers read their instructions from a computer screen and if they needed a hard copy, had it printed out then. Carnes liked to open file folders and flip through the papers as he briefed his officers.

"Got an interesting problem here. Fellow named Rama Lu O'Shaughnessy got himself killed by a robot. Tossed down an elevator shaft without the benefit of the elevator. One of the new 4000 series."

"So?"

"We've got a man dead by violence. A man killed by a robot."

"That's nothing we've got to worry about. Turn it over to the manufacturer and let them determine what happened. Hell, you said that the robot did it. I take it there were witnesses to the act. Why bother us?"

Carnes was quiet for a moment as he stared at Brackett. Finally he said, "You've got to learn to control your mouth, Brackett. You're not here to give advice, or to tell me the obvious. You're here to listen."

"A berserk robot does not fall into our jurisdiction," said Brackett.

"No one said that the robot was berserk," said Carnes tiredly. "I said that it had thrown a man down the elevator shaft."

Brackett shook his head and wished he was in the Off Duty with Jennifer Daily or Sara Cohen or even the robotic marvel that sat outside Carnes's office. He wanted to be anywhere but sitting in Carnes's office listening to the man pontificate. He'd even prefer rotating slowly over an open fire as his juices bubbled from his body.

Carnes shuffled his papers and said, "You might be interested to know that after disposing of Mr. O'Shaughnessy, the robot returned to duty. It attacked the man, that specific man, a man identified as a robed disciple of the Hare O'Shaughnessy splinter group."

"If that's the worst the robot has done, I say more power to it. Maybe we should hire a couple for the space and airports. Keep the freaks from begging . . ."

"Your job," said Carnes, his voice rising, "is not to judge, but to keep the peace."

Brackett grinned, thinking that it was so easy to get under Carnes's skin. The man had no sense of humor. He couldn't see beyond the immediate job, couldn't see the humor in any situation, and was so intense at times that Brackett thought he might burst into flames.

"Still, a robot disposing of a man even if it sounds as if the man deserved to be thrown down the elevator shaft isn't in our jurisdiction."

"It is when it takes place on the ninety-sixth floor of the Star Rest Imperium Hotel with Dennis Profitt in residence at the time."

"Ah, shit!" said Brackett. "Politics."

"If you paid a little more attention to the politics of the situation, you wouldn't be just a lieutenant," said Carnes, staring at Brackett.

"I like being a lieutenant," said Brackett defensively. He waved a hand as if to wipe the thought away. "Besides, this still could be handled by the Special Projects detachment. It falls into their jurisdiction. They can shuttle off to the hotel and get the facts."

"Profitt has made an official request and we're the closest precinct. We've got the call. We'll be in orbit sometime between twenty-four and thirty-six hours from now. By then I want you up to speed on this case. I want you to know everything that has happened, who it happened to, who might have been involved, and why it happened."

"It's not something that we need to do," said Brackett. "It's ridiculous to waste our time on this."

"But waste it we will," said Carnes, his voice hardening, "because Profitt asked for it. You'll be the officer in charge. You have any questions?"

"Why the whole Star Precinct?"

"Because that's what Mr. Profitt would like."

Brackett stood and felt like dumping the desk over on Carnes, just to watch him squirm. Then, for good measure, he'd stomp the holo into rubble.

"You'll report to communications and get everything they have on this. You will be ready when we enter orbit." Carnes folded his arms across his chest as if to say that he had spoken and it was time for his inferiors to obey.

Brackett rubbed a hand through his thinning hair and felt like punching Carnes in his smug face, but knew it would do no good. He'd catch the reprimand and Carnes would probably get promoted.

"Communications," said Brackett.

"They're waiting," said Carnes. He bent back to his important work.

2 | It Was Love at First Sight

Dennis Profitt was the richest human in the known universe. Not the richest being. That honor belonged to something that looked like a slug, but that had found a planet, a moon actually, that seemed to be made out of fissionable material. The slug claimed the moon, and the title of the richest creature in the known universe. Profitt ran a distant second, but didn't care. The slug couldn't communicate with humans, hated the sight of humans, and stayed on the fringes of the galaxy, reaping the wages of its find, leaving Profitt to run his empire.

Profitt sat in his penthouse, on the top of the Star Rest Imperium Hotel, and looked through the bullet-, beam-, laser-, and blast-proof glass. He could look down into a city that had grown up around the mines that produced iridium, a compound that allowed ships to travel faster than the speed of light. That made Profitt the second-richest creature in the known universe.

Profitt was a fairly young man, only forty-five but who looked to be fifty-five, the results of radiation given off by the iridium. He took it in stride because looks weren't important when you could buy people and planets and even whole solar systems.

Not that Profitt wasn't good-looking. He was tall, slender, with only the beginnings of a potbelly that was easily concealed by his clothes. His hair was dark and short, kept that way by a master barber who did nothing but make sure that no gray showed on Profitt's head.

Daily he worked out in a gym equipped with everything that an athlete could want including an instructor who was only too happy to strip her leotard for a little additional instruction in the proper methods of sexual intercourse. She worked at staying appealing for Profitt and he made it worth her while, paying her triple the going rate.

Now he was sitting in a living room the size of a basketball court, a long, tan couch arcing through half the room, a cold glass of vodka in his hand. He swirled the liquid around, letting it soak into the monstrous olive, imported just for him, and stared out through the wall of glass. A red sports job flashed through the sky, came dangerously close to the antiaircraft defenses, and then peeled away leaving a fiery streak in the darkening sky.

Profitt sipped his drink and then glanced to the right, where the numerals giving him the correct time seemed to hover in the air over a small table. To himself, he said, "Now where in the hell is she?"

He stood and yelled, "Klaus? Where are you, Klaus?"

The butler, a young man with huge muscles, a shaved head, and a sinister look, appeared. "Sir?"

"Have you seen Janet?"

"Your wife is in the sauna, sir. Been there for the last hour, I believe."

"Good God," said Profitt. "An hour?"

"Yes, sir. She asked not to be disturbed."

Profitt held out his hand and Klaus took the drink setting it on a tray. "Come along. We're going to be late for dinner. We'll have to hurry her up."

"Yes, sir."

They walked across the living room, down a hall with thick, purple carpet, and reached a wide, circular staircase that took them down to the lower level. They stepped off, onto the wooden tile of the gym. They walked to the sauna. It wasn't a typical sauna because it was as large as a house. There were benches, chairs, a view screen that had access to four hundred twelve separate entertainment, news, and social channels, a shallow pool of warm water, and a larger pool of colder water. A workout area was at the side of the swimming pool, and there were controls that allowed the occupant to regulate just how warm the sauna was. Sometimes Janet allowed the temperature to drop to within a few degrees of eighty.

The first indication they had that something was wrong was that the door was locked. From the inside. The locks had been put there so that Profitt could isolate himself when he wanted. No one else ever used them.

Profitt banged on the door with the palm of his hand. He leaned forward and looked through the small window in the door. It looked as if the interior was deserted.

"Janet," yelled Profitt. "What in the hell are you doing in there?" He shifted around, leaning against the side of the window, trying to get a good look at all sections of the sauna. He couldn't see anything.

Klaus touched the button on the intercom system and said, "Mrs. Profitt? Are you there?"

"Of course she's in there, you idiot," snapped Profitt. "You said she went in."

"Yes, sir," said Klaus.

Profitt grabbed the door handle and shook it. The door was solid. Like it was on a vault. "Come on!" he yelled.

"I'll get a hammer," said Klaus.

"Do it," said Profitt. He moved around and used the security system and view screen to search the interior of the sauna. It was supposed to be able to see into every corner of the sauna, but Profitt couldn't find his wife. She had to be in there, probably with Tony or William. She spent too much time with those two. Men who were closer to her age and who were a little too good-looking for his taste.

He leaned against the intercom and screamed, "If you're screwing around in there, Janet, you're going to be one sorry bitch."

Klaus reappeared with a tool. It was a small claw hammer and not the sledgehammer that Profitt had expected.

"What the hell good is that?"

"I thought I'd break the glass, reach in to the lock. It'll be simple to repair. Cheap."

"Do it," ordered Profitt.

Klaus stepped up, swung the hammer slowly, as if to aim, and then warned, "Please step back, sir."

Profitt turned his face away and closed his eyes. He heard the hammer slam into the glass, and then heard it shatter. As he turned, Klaus was smashing the jagged edges with the side of the hammer. He then stood up on his toes and reached in, groping for the lock.

"That's got it, sir." He threw open the door and danced back, out of the way.

Profitt rushed in, surveyed the sauna, but couldn't see his wife. "She's not here, you dummy."

Klaus stood at the door, the hammer in his hand, and didn't move.

Profitt walked toward the pool, looked at the tables and chairs arranged around it, and thought that something didn't look right. Something was out of place.

And then he spotted her, lying between two of the benches. Lying on her back, staring up at the overhead lights, and not moving. He started toward her. "Janet? What in the hell is going on here?"

Klaus joined him as they reached Janet. She was naked, her skin a bright pink from the excess heat in the sauna. Her eyes were open, her mouth slack. There was a single drop of blood in the corner of her eye, looking like a small crimson tear.

Profitt knelt near her head and touched her cheek. "Janet?" he said again, his voice quiet. "Janet?"

Klaus reached down and took her wrist, searching for a pulse with his fingers.

Profitt pushed him away. "Don't touch her. You're not supposed to touch her." Then, seeming to notice for the first time that she was completely naked, he screamed, "Stop looking at her!"

Backpedaling, Klaus stood up, but couldn't pull his eyes away from the body. It was the first time that he'd seen someone dead except on the video and that didn't count. He'd never been in the same room with, let alone touched, a dead body. He noticed that his fingers were tingling. He shook them, as if there was water on them.

"Janet," said Profitt, "enough of this nonsense. Get up and get dressed or we'll be late."

She didn't move. She didn't blink. She didn't breathe.

Klaus returned carrying a towel. He spread it on her carefully, covering her from the top of her head to her thighs. Then he reached down and tugged at Profitt, trying to get him to stand.

"Sir, we must call the police."

"The police are on the way," said Profitt. "Star Precinct 107."

"The local police," said Klaus. "We must call the local police."

Profitt staggered back and sat down on one of the benches. His clothes were soaked with sweat but he didn't notice the heat. He hunched over, his elbows on his knees, and stared at the body of his wife.

"What happened?" he asked.

"Sir, I have got to call the police. Will you be all right here?"

Profitt waved a hand. "Go." Then unaware that Klaus had obeyed the order, he asked, "What could have happened to her? I don't understand."

He didn't know how long he sat there, looking down at her. She had been a pretty thing. Young, brunette this week, tanned, alive. Sometimes she seemed empty-headed, unable to follow the simplest line of reasoning, but then Profitt hadn't married her for her brains. She was decorative, the type of woman who turned the heads of everything male in the room. There was an aura about her. Something that caught everyone's attention.

Profitt had bought her just as he'd bought everything else that he'd wanted. First he'd negotiated with her father, settling nearly half a million on him to buy his silence, if not his approval. Then he'd put a million two in a special bank account just for her. Money that she wouldn't have to touch unless she wanted it. A nest egg. A security blanket, in case she decided that he was too repulsive to stay around any longer.

That had bought her affection, if not her undying love. It was an arrangement that Profitt could tolerate. And no one else had to know the arrangements of the purchase.

"Sir," said Klaus, "the police are here."

Profitt stood and turned to find two uniformed officers and one plainclothes detective standing at the edge of the pool, looking down at the body. One of them had a cigarette in his mouth, surprising Profitt. Almost no one smoked anymore. Too dangerous.

"That your wife?" asked the man in plainclothes. Plain clothes was the right term. A gray suit that needed to be pressed, a white shirt that showed the man had eaten something brown for lunch, and a wrinkled tie pulled down. He was almost a video version of a cop.

"Who are you?" asked Profitt.

"Detective Sergeant Hughes."

"Well, Detective," said Profitt, his voice stronger now, "that indeed is my wife."

"She dead?"

"Yes."

"How?"

"I don't know. She was locked in here, was late coming out. We had to break in."

"You touch anything?"

"No."

Klaus spoke up. "We covered her with the towel. Didn't seem right leaving her . . . like she was."

"Wished you hadn't done that," said Hughes.

Profitt looked at the other two police officers and noticed that one was a woman. Long hair and a narrow face.

"Do you need us here any longer?" asked Klaus.

"No. Don't leave the apartment."

Klaus said, "Mr. Profitt, maybe we should go upstairs and allow the officers to do their jobs."

"We'll have some questions for you a little later," said Hughes.

"Should I have my attorney present?" asked Profitt.

"Now there's an interesting question," said Hughes. "Why would you want your attorney?"

"Whenever I have dealings with police officials, I find it helpful to have my attorney present."

"The innocent man has no need of legal counsel," said Hughes.

"Everyone, when dealing with the police, has need of legal counsel," said Profitt. He turned to go, stopped, and took a final glance at the female officer, noticing that her build was reminiscent of Janet's, that her legs looked strong yet very feminine.

"We'll be up to talk to you in a few minutes," said Hughes.

"Thank you, Officer," said Klaus.

Profitt started toward the door but stopped at one of the tables. He took a towel and wiped the sweat from his face. Looking at Klaus, he asked, "What do you think happened to her?"

"Too much heat," he said. "Must have caused a heart attack."

"She looked so peaceful," said Profitt. "So very peaceful." With that he walked out, into the cooler air of the penthouse.

3 | The Cops Are in the Donut Shop

Jennifer Daily had tired of her word processor and imagined crimes. She'd tired of making up tales that involved murder and rape and naked women that would appeal to the producers of the various vidjournals and vidscreen plays. The make-believe mayhem was getting to her in a way that the real mayhem never did and she suspected that it was because the make-believe was coming from inside her. That scared her. Just a little. She wondered if she might not have a dark side that would enjoy creating some of the mayhem for real.

She left her office and walked down to the Cup and Hole for some coffee and a donut. She picked up a pastry, pushed a cup under the spigot of the machine, and let it fill it. She then moved to one of the tables and sat down, looking out into space.

The view was so peaceful. A solid black backdrop filled with brilliant points of light. She turned her attention to the donut, pulling it apart so that it was bite-sized. Between bites, she sipped the coffee.

Tate entered, spotted her, and made a beeline for her. "Mind if I join you?"

"No."

Tate pulled out the chair and dropped into it. "Brackett's got his ass in the sling."

She shifted her attention from space and her donut so that she could look at him. "Now why would you say that?"

"Carnes was after him. Searching for him and leaving messages for him to report to the upper level just as quickly as he could."

"Doesn't mean he's in trouble. There are a hundred things that Carnes could want."

Tate leaned forward, his elbows on the tabletop. "You ever know Carnes to have anything good to say to the loot? Five'll get you twenty that Brackett's had his ass handed to him."

Daily took the last bite of donut and then patted her lips to remove any crumbs. "Do I detect a note of self-satisfaction in that analysis?"

"Hell, no. I like the loot. He's square with me. Helps when he can. I'm just making an observation."

"Maybe I should go see if I can find him."

Tate ignored that and asked, "You have any idea where we're heading?"

"Nope. Thought that we were on routine patrol, next stop Bolton's Planet."

"Course was changed," said Tate. "Couple of hours ago. We're now heading elsewhere though the navigation and flight crews won't tell me where we're going."

"Security regulations," said Daily automatically.

"Right. Like I'm going to spread the word to those who are not authorized to know. Like there are any who aren't supposed to know."

"Way it's always been," said Daily, standing. She brushed the crumbs from the front of her uniform, adjusted the leather of her gunbelt, shifted her handcuff case, and straightened her tie.

"Priming for your meeting with the loot?"

"You know, Tate, sometimes you don't have the brains it'd take to blow yourself up." With that, she strode out of the Cup and Hole.

Brackett left Carnes's office in a murderous rage. Just seeing the man did that to him. Sometimes, late at night, in his quarters as he dreamed about his late wife and Janos, he couldn't remember what Janos had looked like. Janos's face disappeared, replaced by Carnes. The two great nemeses of his life were Janos and Carnes and they seemed to be interchangeable.

The elevator took him down to the communications and research centers. He walked into the brightly lighted areas. Neither looked like what it was. The communications center was not alive with radios, videos, subspace, and hyperspace communicators. The research facility looked nothing like a library or archive. All information was accessed through computer terminals hooked into the mainframe hidden from the view of everyone except the four-person crew whose only job was to keep it functioning and to prevent sabotage.

Brackett blinked at the brightness of the lights in the research center. He walked across the thick carpet that had been treated to prevent a buildup of static electricity. He sat down at one of the terminals, touched the metallic disk on the table that was supposed to prevent static discharge near the keyboards, and then laced his fingers, bending them back like a concert pianist about to launch into a classical program.

One of the clerks appeared next to him and asked, "Something we can help you with, Loot?"

"Nah," said Brackett, looking up. The clerk was a cadaverous man with pasty skin and stringy hair. There were black circles under his eyes making his face look like an animated skull. "I can handle it myself."

"If you need anything, let me know." He whirled and hurried off.

Brackett sat for a moment and smiled to himself. What he should be doing was sitting in communications, reading the traffic about the robot-caused death. He shouldn't be in the research center about to tap the mainframe with questions about Dennis Profitt.

He sat for a moment, staring at the blank screen, and then typed, "Dennis Profitt . . . human . . . male . . . Terran."

The screen flashed "Accessing" at him and a moment later, the data, including a picture of Profitt, appeared. The picture rotated, right and left slowly, so that Brackett could get a good look at the man.

He touched a button and the picture faded and the text began to slowly scroll. He gave all the vital statistics such as date of birth: June 25, '76; place of birth: Denver, New Colony, Earth. Schooling was normal and included two years of mining training after high school. Nothing spectacular. Nothing to show how Profitt had become the second-richest creature in the known universe.

Brackett skipped the preliminaries, searching for the meat of the biography. He scrolled down rapidly, scanning, and then stopped as the information began to interest him.

He learned that at twenty-one, Profitt and two companions, Jason Argon and David Kincaid, had shipped out, or rather had pooled their limited resources to purchase a used ship. They went deeply into debt to retrofit it with the latest in computer and navigation equipment, and like the youngsters of a hundred other generations set out to make their fortune.

Not much was known, for certain, about the next six years, though Profitt's autobiography (available as a talking book, video version, or accessible under Profitt, bio, auto) claimed that he and his friends prospected their way through a number of star systems until they struck it rich. Argon was killed by a carnivorous beast and the radiation that had made Profitt sick had killed Kincaid.

But the strike was worth the cost, and Profitt emerged as the richest creature in the known universe, until the appearance of the intelligent slug a decade later. Profitt had been near the planet that slug had found and could have made the same discovery as the slug, but the importance of that ore wouldn't be learned until five years after Profitt returned from space.

Idly, Brackett wondered about the tragedy that fell on the tiny band of explorers. Of course, there were hundreds of ships that had left Earth, Mars, Tau Ceti Four, Sirius Two and Three, Vega Twelve, and a dozen other places that had never been seen again. Heading out into relatively uncharted space was a hazard. Even today, charted space was hazardous. There were ion storms, floating debris, and even a few pirates that caused the disappearance of ships. Help was often weeks away if it was available at all.

Profitt had lived relatively quietly since his return from space. He finally moved to the planet where he and his friends had made their discovery, setting himself up as a kind of king. He could do no wrong because the two million residents in the main city made their livings in industries directly related to Profitt's find.

There was nothing to suggest that Profitt was an evil man or even a mildly irritating one. He was one of the lucky few to have made a fortune so vast that there was nothing that he would ever want. To Brackett's way of thinking, that didn't make Profitt bad. Just lucky.

He scrolled through more of the documentation available, but mostly it was vid-hype of Profitt. Profitt establishing a children's hospital. Profitt endowing a foundation to eliminate racial hatred. Profitt giving money so that the starving hordes on Deneb Six, who weren't even human, but were intelligent, could be fed and saved.

Profitt was a "goody-two-shoes" who apparently didn't have the intelligence to become rich, but was lucky enough to stumble into it. There had been hundreds of them in the past. Men and women who despite everything had made money.

Brackett took a deep breath and exhaled slowly. Nothing to suggest that anyone would want to kill Profitt, though a rich man had enemies he didn't know. Of course, Carnes hadn't said that Profitt was the target, just that he was in residence at the hotel where the attack had taken place. Maybe he was reading too much into the random act of a malfunctioning robot.

He cleared the screen and stood up. The clerk came from his glass-enclosed booth and asked, "Anything else we can do for you, Loot?"

"Nope. Got what I want. Thanks."

"Thank you." He hurried toward the table that Brackett had just vacated, checking to make sure that everything was as it was supposed to be. Brackett wondered if the man was real or artificial. Some of the artificials were so good that it was impossible to tell for certain.

In the corridor, walking toward the communications center, he was stopped by Daily. She sneaked up on him and asked abruptly, "Carnes chew on you?"

He started and knew that Daily had done it on purpose. It was a game she played since the first day they had met. She'd appeared behind him, touched his shoulder, and Brackett had nearly decked her in automatic response.

"No. New assignment. I guess you'll be included too. This one is all politics."

"Where are you going?"

"Communications to take a look at the package. You want to come along?"

"Sure. Might as well get up to speed as quickly as possible. This explain the course change?"

Brackett laughed. "Scuttlebutt gets around quickly."

"Tate said that we'd changed course but he didn't know the destination."

They reached the communications center and the hatch irised open for them. Brackett stepped through, moved to the side, and waited for Daily. He let her lead him to the counter where they would speak to the watch officer. Brackett wanted her to lead for two reasons. One was so that she couldn't surprise him again. And the other was so he could watch her walk. In the tight, short uniform skirt, it was a sight to behold. He'd never mentioned that to her because he didn't want to be labeled as a male chauvinistic pig. He tried not to look, but sometimes he couldn't resist it.

"Help you?" asked the woman behind the counter.

"Need to see the message traffic, bulletins, and Form Fives that deal with the robot-involved death at the Star Rest Imperium."

"Classified," said the clerk.

"Hell," said Brackett, grinning, "do you think we'd be down here asking you these question if we weren't authorized the information?"

"No, Loot, I guess not. Have a seat and I'll bring the stuff to you."

"Not on the computer?"

"Nope. Haven't got it logged in. Most of it came by courier. I'll bring it over."

Brackett and Daily moved toward one of the tables. The communications center was as brightly lighted as the research facility. The area was large with lots of what Brackett considered wasted space. Open deck covered with a dark carpeting. Bulkheads painted in earth tones. The quiet chirping of the various communications devices muffled by the soundproofing. Brackett had been told that the communications center had been designed for the expansion of equipment as modifications were made and more communications gear was needed, but that hadn't happened. The improved technology hadn't taken more space but less.

The clerk appeared and set the printouts on the table. She added a minicomputer to the stack. "That'll clarify a few things. Contains data on the hotel to include blueprints, history of the hotel and the city, and a listing of the hotel staff. The nice-to-know information."

"Thanks." Brackett picked up the printout and left the minicomputer to Daily. Her training in sociology and psychology made that the assignment for her.

Brackett worked his way through the paper quickly, being careful to maintain the fanfolds in the proper order. Finished, he dropped the printout on the table and rocked back, his fingers laced behind his head. He closed his eyes momentarily to rest them.

"Routine," he said.

Looking up from the minicomputer screen, Daily said, "Nothing of interest here. No sudden staff changes, good background checks on them all, and limited access to the upper floors."

"The only question is why the robot would go berserk, attack a single individual, and then return to its duties," said Brackett.

"The answer is obvious," said Daily. "It was just doing its job."

4 | The Shadows of Night

Detective Sergeant Hughes had left the sauna because his heart was beginning to hammer, his suit was sweat-soaked, and his shirt was wringing wet. He staggered to the circular steps and sat down hard, grabbing at the railing.

The female uniformed officer, wearing standard issue of dark, long-sleeved shirt, black tie, and narrow, midthigh-length skirt, followed him. "You okay, Sarge?"

"You're new, aren't you . . .?"

"Denise OBrien, Sarge. Three months."

"Well, OBrien, I hate being called Sarge. Detective. Tom. Or even Hughes. But not Sarge."

"Sorry."

He looked up at her. She looked as hot as he did. Her face was flushed and there were beads of sweat on her upper lip and along her hairline. "Who's your partner?"

"Frank Ryan."

Hughes leaned to the left, to look around her and at the door, and raised his voice. "Ryan! Get out here."

Ryan appeared a moment later looking like a cat that had just escaped the rain. His hair, sweat-damp, hung in his face. His uniform shirt was soaked and clinging to his chest.

"Just what were you doing in there?" asked Hughes.

"Securing the crime scene, Sarge."

Hughes shot a glance at OBrien and knew that she would brief him the first chance she got. To Ryan, he said, "Okay, here's the skinny. I want you to go upstairs and find that Klaus guy and question him. Out of earshot of Mr. Profitt." He turned to look at OBrien. "You question Mr. Profitt. Find out everything you can about what happened. Gently."

"Wouldn't Frank be better for that?"

"No," said Hughes. "First, because I set the assignments the way I wanted them, but second, and more importantly, I saw the way he studied you. He might let his guard down a little more with a pretty officer questioning him. Let's play to his weakness."

"Sure, Tom."

Hughes stood up and then said, "And I'm not sure about that Klaus fellow. He looks like a rough customer and he might like boys better than girls. We'll have to see about that."

"What are you going to do?" asked OBrien.

"First, I'm going up there with you to make sure that we get things set the way I want them, then I'm going to find a drink of water before I come back down here. I want to inspect the crime scene carefully."

"Shouldn't one of us remain here to secure it?" asked Ryan.

"From whom? This is a security penthouse. No one's going to wander in without alerting everyone. Besides, I'm not sure that there's much in the way of evidence to be preserved anyway."

"You're the boss, Sarge," said Ryan.

Hughes turned and walked up the stairs slowly, thinking that they were wider than his living room and had they been level, he could have fit most of his apartment on them. The rich lived different from the rest of humanity.

They reached the upper level and walked down a hall that could have doubled for a tennis court. If the carpet had been green instead of purple, Hughes could have used it as a putting green. Hell, he could have used it as a par three hole.

They exited into the living room. Profitt was sitting on the couch, staring out into the deepening dusk. Klaus stood to one side, out of Profitt's sight, waiting for orders.

"I'm afraid that there are some questions that have to be asked," said Hughes to announce their arrival.

Profitt stood and turned. "Now?"

"Routine," said Hughes. "Mr. Profitt, Officer OBrien will speak with you. Officer Ryan will take your servant into another room."

"I'm not sure that I want to answer questions yet," said Profitt.

Hughes guided OBrien around the end of the couch and had her sit down. She brushed a hand through her rapidly drying hair, and then pulled a notebook from her pocket. She crossed her legs slowly, letting her skirt ride higher. Profitt noticed that.

"Just let her ask the questions. You're under no obligation to answer them. You can decide. Of course, if you've nothing to hide, then you shouldn't mind."

"I've called for my attorney," said Profitt.

"Well, it's up to you. Officer Ryan, you may take the servant into another room." Hughes kept his eyes on Profitt to gauge his reaction.

"Go ahead, Klaus."

"Yes, sir."

"Now," said Hughes, "I'd like some water."

Profitt pointed at a door. "There is a small kitchen through there. You'll find water there."

"Thank you." Hughes turned and walked quickly to the kitchen. He pushed on the door, entered, and then stopped. Profitt's idea of small didn't match his own. This would be suitable for a restaurant.

He found a sink and noticed that one of the taps was labeled for ice water. He opened a cupboard, found a glass, and filled it with the ice water. It was cold enough to make his teeth ache and send slivers of pain through his head. He decided that the label wasn't to announce the tap had ice water, it was to warn everyone about the ice water.

He took another drink and poured the rest of the water into the sink. Leaving the kitchen, he saw that OBrien had Profitt on the couch talking to her. He didn't wait to see if he was answering the questions. He hurried down the hall and descended the stairs to the sauna.

He entered and stopped short. There was a man standing near the body of Janet Profitt. A tall man, in tailored, expensive clothes. A distinguished man with graying hair.

"Just who in the hell are you?" said Hughes.

The man jumped, startled, and then turned. "I'm sorry. I was to have dinner with the Profitts."

"How'd you get in here," asked Hughes, aware that the man hadn't answered the first question.

"What happened here? Is that Mrs. Profitt? Is she dead?"

Hughes advanced on the man, thinking that he looked familiar. He was slender with broad shoulders and long legs. The gray trousers contrasted to his dark suit coat, snow-white shirt, and dark, probably navy, tie.

"I'm Detective Sergeant Hughes, and I must have some answers to my questions."

"You have credentials?" asked the man.

That stopped Hughes. He wasn't used to being questioned by civilians. Especially civilians who were found at the scene of a possible crime. But, without thinking, he reached into his hip pocket and produced the wallet that held his badge and holo ID. He flipped it open and showed it to the man.

"Sorry, Detective. My name is Ambassador Sumner Gleason. I have a dinner engagement here." He stressed the word "ambassador" as if to tell Hughes just how important he was. He stared at the detective, waiting for him to look away.

"How did you get in?"

"Hotel staff knows me, of course. I noticed the door to the sauna was open and walked in."

"Yeah. How come no one announced you?"

"I'm sure they did."

"How come you're down here and not upstairs in that fancy living room?"

"Am I a suspect, Officer?"

"You are now," said Hughes. "I find you at the crime scene. You become a suspect."

"There has been a crime?"

Hughes wiped his face with his left hand and stuffed his badge back into his pocket. That was the one thing that hadn't been determined. Mrs. Profitt was dead, but no one had determined if she had died by violence, by the hand of another human, or if she had just died.

Hughes stepped over one of the benches and sat down. He stared at Janet Profitt's feet and then her legs. He glanced back at the ambassador. He then crouched near her and pulled the towel away from the body.

"Must you do that?" asked Gleason.

"Yeah," said Hughes. He stood up, the towel in his hand. "Good-looking broad, don't you think?"

"I find that remark in the poorest of taste."

Hughes dropped the towel and then knelt near her head. He bent close and inspected her face. He reached down and touched the bridge of her nose. He scrambled around and it looked as if he were about to kiss her forehead.

"Must you do that?" asked Gleason again.

Hughes ignored him. He inspected her face, lifted an eyelid, and then rocked back on his heels. He touched the side of her throat and then looked down at her chest, studying her body carefully. He did touch her shoulder, lifted her slightly, and looked at the floor under her back.

"Sergeant!"

"Detective," said Hughes. He grabbed the towel and draped it over her body again.

He stood up and looked at Gleason. "Now, Mr. Ambassador, maybe we'd better head on upstairs and talk to Mr. Profitt."

"I think you're right. I'm going to inform Mr. Profitt about your actions here."

"Please do. And I'll be checking your story out. I find it more than a little interesting that you were standing over the body."

"You said that a crime hadn't been committed here."

"No, I don't believe that's what I said." He held out a hand and said, "After you, Mr. Ambassador."

"You're going to leave her here?"

"She's not going anywhere," said Hughes. "And I don't want anything touched until the whole area is photographed and videotaped."

"I think I'll be mentioning your conduct to your superiors."

Hughes waited until the ambassador had walked out of the sauna. He then closed the door to the sauna and looked at the broken window.

Together they climbed the stairs. They walked down the hall and entered the living room. OBrien and Profitt were still sitting on the couch, but now there were lights on casting a few shadows. Profitt had turned so that he was facing the police officer.

"Dennis," said the ambassador, "I've just learned about the tragedy." He hurried forward, a hand out to be shaken. "I can't tell you how sorry I am."

Profitt stood and turned. "Sumner. I'm sorry. I completely forgot about . . ."

"That's not important." The ambassador advanced across the room. "I'm so very sorry."

"Thank you. We don't know what happened. It's a shock. Surprise . . . I don't know."

Hughes looked at OBrien. "Have you finished?"

"Yes, Tom. I'm . . ."

"Fine. Head downstairs and secure the sauna until the lab people, the coroner, and the video crew arrive."

"Yes, sir."

Hughes moved forward, closer to the ambassador and Profitt. "Excuse me, but word of this is going to get out in a few minutes. There are going to be vid freaks all over the place. You'll be on the news in fifteen minutes."

"There are people who will take care of that," said Profitt.

"Yes, sir, I thought so," said Hughes. "Which reminds me. How did the ambassador get by all those people?"

"Oh, for God's sake," said Profitt. "They know that the ambassador was expected. They'd clear him up here without any hassle."

"If you'll be all right," said Hughes, "I've work to do."

"Certainly," said Profitt.

"I would appreciate it if you'd remain in the penthouse. I'm sure that we'll have additional questions."

"Maybe you should alert your attorney," said Gleason.

Hughes shook his head. "Mrs. Profitt is dead and everyone wants to call for an attorney. Interesting."

"I don't care for your tone," said the ambassador.

"Yes, well." Hughes turned, crossed the floor, and rapped on the door to the room where Ryan was questioning Klaus. "Meet me in the sauna when you're finished."

"Sure . . . Tom."

Hughes headed back downstairs. He saw that OBrien was standing outside the sauna, her back to it. He sat down on the bottom step, stared at her for a moment, and asked, "What'd you learn?"

"They, meaning Profitt and Klaus, went in search of the wife because they had to get ready for a dinner meeting. Klaus said that he saw her go into the sauna."

"Making him the last one to see her alive?"

"Maybe. Anyway, found that the sauna was locked. From the inside. They had to break the window to get in. Found her lying between the benches. Just where we saw her. Klaus put the towel on her. That's all they know."

Hughes took a deep breath and wiped a hand through his hair. "Doesn't make much sense. A young woman just doesn't drop dead. There has to be a reason. Drugs? Booze? There has to be something."

OBrien shrugged. "The heat? Spend too long in the sauna and it can kill."

"A young, healthy woman? Nah." He hung his head and studied the wooden floor between his feet. It looked like it belonged to basketball courts he'd seen on the sportsvid. "I hope the medics can come up with something."

"Oh," said OBrien. "Profitt told me that he'd called for a Star Precinct."

"What the hell for?"

"Wanted the experts, I guess."

"You know the definition of an expert, don't you? Someone

who lives more than a hundred klicks away and has his own video presentation. Fucking Star Cops. When he'd make that call?"

"This afternoon sometime."

Hughes snorted. "Fucking Star Cops."

5 | Space . . . the Final Frontier

They were more than twelve hours from their destination. The instant they arrived and established their parking orbit, Brackett and his team would be shuttled down to the planet's surface to take over the investigation of a robot that had gone momentarily berserk. All because the second-richest creature in the entire known universe was involved. Or was close. Or had seen the story on the news vids. Or some damned thing.

Brackett sat in the Off Duty, at a small table shoved into the rear corner, where he liked to be because he could see everything that was going on and where the shadows and the various equipment and booths tended to hide him. Sitting across from him was Daily with some type of drink that had a lot of fruit pulp in it, a tiny plastic parasol, a plastic sword that skewered an olive, and a red cherry, slice of lemon, and another piece of plastic that Brackett couldn't identify easily.

Brackett himself had a martini with a twist and no ice. A simple and straightforward drink. He tasted it, nodded his approval, and then set it carefully on the table. He felt that he should say something, but couldn't think of what it should be. Instead he turned his attention to the Off-Duty.

It was the most popular of the three lounges aboard the 107th. Music blared from speakers. Colored lights flashed in time to the music. There was a dance floor that provided an excuse for the patrons to touch one another, a long bar that looked like something from a disco built in the latter half of the twentieth century, a video wall that sometimes showed news, sometimes showed a game, and sometimes showed a video. Most of the videos involved a lot of nudity.

That was the thing about the 107th. It was more than just a police precinct. It was a city drifting in space, following a prescribed orbit through several inhabited solar systems. They sometimes were pulled off their routine to handle special assignments.

But the 107th employed people who were not involved in police work. They were the cooks, the sanitation workers, those who owned the stores, the boutiques, the vid centers, the gaming centers, and the bars. There were those who maintained the ship, who navigated, who piloted, and who controlled it. There were the researchers who staffed the various libraries and research centers, who operated the communications center, and who serviced all the electronics. A large part of the population was lab technicians, forensic experts, medical examiners, and other specialists whose job was the study of evidence gathered by the patrol officers and investigators. There were even those who seemed to have no function in the 107th but who wandered the corridors, and who lived on the very edge of the society. And there was the dark side. The holding cells, the prison facility, and the morgue. Only about ten percent of the people of the 107th were Star Cops.

The 107th was a modern city that floated through space to provide a service to the planets that couldn't afford the technology, or the expertise, that was required of a modern police force.

Leaning forward slightly, Daily said, "I guess I'm surprised that they're diverting the whole precinct rather than just dispatching a shuttle for this case."

"You know," said Brackett, "that was the argument that I made with Carnes, but policy is set at a much higher level. Profitt is a very powerful man and he could easily pay all expenses incurred by us for the diversion and for this investigation."

"So we operate in the black, becoming a profit-making organization."

Brackett rocked back and picked up his martini, draining it. He slammed the glass to the table. "I think I'll go catch a few winks."

"Night's young," said Daily.

"Twelve hours until we've got to get to work," said Brackett.

"So we've got plenty of time," said Daily.

"I want a chance to brief Obo before we hit the field. He doesn't know that we're about to deploy."

"Tomorrow," said Daily. She raised a hand and a slender, polished aluminum robot appeared that was vaguely human. The voice was husky, breathless, and feminine. "Hit us again," Daily ordered.

The robot's sensors determined what each had been drinking and worked away for a moment. The drinks appeared up through the bottom of a thick tray it held. It bent at the waist, holding the tray like a French maid at the dinner table so that Daily could remove the glasses.

"Credit my account," she said.

The robot nodded and whirled away.

Brackett picked up his drink, sipped it, and then laughed. "Exactly the same as the last one."

"You know, Loot," said Daily, feeling reckless, "you should get out with the troops more. You've become a real grind."

Brackett looked at Daily closely. He studied her face and her eyes. The strobing of the lights created patterns and lines that sometimes gave her a nightmarish appearance, and at others made her look almost angelic. The management had planned it that way. They didn't want anyone to look too good or too bad because that tended to hurt business.

"Sometimes," said Brackett slowly, as if feeling out each of the words, "there is nothing other than the job. We have the opportunity here to do some real good for everyone. Not just the human race, but all intelligent life."

"Christ, you sound like a recruiting vid. Join the Star Cops and save humanity. Explore the fringes of the known galaxy and bring law and order to the raw frontier."

Brackett grinned sheepishly and realized that he'd fallen into his defensive mode. When anyone probed too deeply, or seemed to be getting too close, he drifted away and trotted out the standard line about making the known galaxy safe for humanity. What he was really trying to do was make a little piece of it safe for young mothers and their unborn children.

"You know, Loot, I never see you relaxing. I don't think you'd be here if I hadn't insisted."

Brackett raised his glass and said, "And I thank you for insisting. Sometimes I just don't know what's good for me. Or what I need."

"Obo said that you worked too hard but that you'd always been that way."

"Not always," said Brackett. "There was a time when I searched for the shortcut. Clear the job and move on to the next regardless of the circumstance."

Daily nodded, thinking that she knew what he was talking about. The young Star Cop who wanted to rack up results regardless of the techniques needed to do it. Good statistics made for quick promotions and rapid advancement until they reached the upper level where life was good.

Brackett, of course, was talking about his young days as a hustler and con man. Take from the rich and give to the poor, though the poor was him and his wife and his partners, when he had them. He grinned, figuring that it was something that Daily didn't have to know.

Then, almost as if reading his mind, she asked, "How come you never married?"

"That's a tad bit personal."

"Sure, but we're partners. We work together." She touched her glass. "We drink together. Sometimes. And I don't know that much about you."

"I was married once . . . It didn't work out."

"Job got in the way?" asked Daily.

Brackett nodded. "Something like that." He felt a cold chill on his back and his belly had turned to ice. He had to turn the topic quickly. He leaned forward, touched her hand with his fingers, figuring that she'd pull away. She surprised him when she didn't.

Still trying to divert the conversation, he asked, "How goes it with the great police novel?"

Daily picked up her drink, pushed the parasol to one side, sipped, and then pulled the sword with a salad on it out. She bent over the table to keep the liquor from dripping on her, and ate the olive and the lemon.

"I don't know," she said finally. "There's something about it that bothers me. It seems that I'm having too much fun inventing the clever ways to dispatch other intelligences." She looked at him quickly and let her eyes slide away. "And the sex scenes are getting too . . . I don't know . . . hot. Makes me wonder if there isn't some hidden desire in me to try some of the things that I'm making up."

"The crimes or the sex?" asked Brackett without thinking about it.

Now she focused her attention on him. She locked eyes with him and stared, almost as if trying to read his thoughts. "The sex," she said.

Brackett was suddenly uncomfortable again, but this time it wasn't the lousy past. It was the possibility of a bright and glowing future. He hesitated just an instant and said, "Anything interesting?"

"Something called the basket," she said, her voice slipping an octave lower. She closed her eyes momentarily, as if she could see it. "Involves a hook on the ceiling, stirrups for the feet, and the man on the bottom."

Brackett found that he couldn't quite visualize what she meant but he decided that he wasn't going to ask. That question was too loaded.

"The woman spins around, just over . . ."

"I think I get the picture," said Brackett, not sure at all. But he didn't want to talk about it.

Daily picked up her drink and sipped at it for a moment. She kept her eyes on him, watching him. Finally she put down the glass and said, "I think that I'm finished here."

Brackett glanced up at one of the ship's chronometers and noticed that nearly an hour had passed. He couldn't believe that time was getting away from him. It had seemed that it was only seconds. Only a few minutes. There was work to do, there were documents and reports to be studied, and he needed to get some rest before they shuttled down.

"I think that I'd like to head back to my cabin," said Daily. "Would you care to join me?"

Brackett shrugged, unsure of what to say. He just sat there, struck dumb.

"Don't you find me attractive?"

"You've very good-looking," said Brackett lamely.

"Then let's go. No reason that we shouldn't share a little . . ."

"There are the lines of authority," said Brackett quickly. "I am your superior officer. Directly in your chain of command. There could be those who would suggest that I, as your superior, ah, induced . . ."

"Oh, don't be stupid," said Daily. "You've never been anything other than the perfect gentleman. You've treated me fairly, as a police officer and not as a . . . what? Stupid woman? I find you to be . . ."

Brackett glanced up then and saw Obo enter the Off-Duty. It was hard not to see him. He towered over most of the people, over the decorations and the speakers and even the tops of the booths designed to provide maximum privacy. He was like a beacon on the shore on a cloudless night.

Obo knew that Brackett liked to hide in the back and moved through the crowd toward the rear. He raised a huge hand to let Brackett see him.

"I come in search of you," said Obo.

Brackett pointed at one of the chairs and asked, "Would you care to join us?" He wasn't sure that he was glad that Obo had arrived but he was grateful for the opportunity to think about what Daily had said.

"Obo will sit, but only for a short time."

"Would you care for a drink?" asked Brackett. He saw Daily roll her eyes as if to ask, "What in the hell are you doing here?"

"No drink. Alcohol just makes illness." Obo tried to smile, but it was more of a sneer. Those who didn't know him, or the members of his race, sometimes thought that he was about to attack.

"What can we do for you, Obo?" asked Daily.

"Captain Carnes has a desire to see you, Loot. He has come in search of you. He has sent me out in search of you. To find you and tell you this thing."

"I spoke to him earlier. Learned that we've got an assignment coming up."

"Yes, but he comes and looks again," said Obo. He blinked rapidly, signaling that he was unhappy with delivering the bad news.

"Looks like you've been saved by a higher authority," said Daily.

"I wish you wouldn't look at it like that," responded Brackett.

"I'll be in my cabin," said Daily. She finished her drink quickly and stood up suddenly. "I'll be there for the rest of the night."

"I'll remember that," said Brackett.

Daily turned and then slowly walked from the Off-Duty. At the door she stopped and glanced back. Then, without waving, she disappeared.

"Obo should not have come."

"No, Obo, you did right. I assume that Carnes told you that we're landing tomorrow."

"Yes. Ready to go."

Now Brackett stood. "I don't know what Carnes could possibly want now. He's already briefed me."

"Captain Carnes say he wait for you in the Cup and Hole. He go off-duty now."

"Thanks, Obo," said Brackett. He left the Off-Duty.

6 | The Day After the Night Before

Brackett, Daily, Obo, and Tate, who'd realized that a story involving the second-richest creature in the known universe was worth exploring, sat at one of the round tables in the rear of the tiny shuttle. The parking orbit had been established on time, the shuttle had been ready on time, and Carnes had been standing in the shuttle bay to remind them a final time that Profitt was extremely rich and powerful. To fuck up here was to fuck up truly, for all times, near and far.

Brackett had grinned and said, "Thanks for the support, Captain. I know that I and the rest of my team appreciate your taking the time to come down here and tell us that our lives are about to end."

"That's not what I said."

"Close enough." Brackett looked at his team, and then at the shuttle crew that was working to get ready for the flight. "I guess we can board."

Carnes moved closer, lowered his voice, and said, "The opposite of finding yourself on the outs is to solve the riddle here and move into the limelight. Those who succeed can find their path paved with gold."

"That a subtle bribe?" asked Daily.

"No, Sergeant, it is a statement of fact." Carnes's voice became hard. "If you people paid just the slightest attention to the political aspects of some of your cases, you'd find that the road to the top was a lot smoother."

"Fuck it," said Brackett. He turned and looked at the shuttle. The hatch was open, beckoning them forward.

They had entered, buckled into the plush, wraparound seats, and waited for the shuttle to drop into space. There were ports, but all were closed for that first few frightening minutes of weightlessness as the shuttle moved away from the 107th's gravitational influence.

As soon as the interior lights had come up, Brackett had said, "New information from last night." He glanced at Tate and added, "This is not for attribution yet."

"We're on the record here," said Tate, trying to muscle his way past Brackett.

"Nope. We're off the record or else you're at another table with headphones playing Montavoni so that you can't eavesdrop on us."

"Off the record," agreed Tate. "For the moment."

"Okay. Here's the deal. Our assignment has changed a little. Turns out that some of the research that Sergeant Daily and I did yesterday is going to be a lot more valuable than I had originally thought."

"Sergeant Daily?" said Tate.

"Jennifer," said Brackett.

"Just surprised that she had changed from Jennifer to Sergeant Daily overnight."

"Tate," said Daily, "you're becoming a real pain in the ass. Don't make us sorry that we allowed you to tag along."

"You couldn't have stopped me."

"Well," said Brackett, "that's not exactly true. We could have kept you off this shuttle. Obo would have been more than happy to stand in the way. By the time you could have gotten to Carnes, we'd have been long gone."

Tate looked at the big alien, saw him sneer, and wondered if he was smiling.

"Point made," said Tate.

Brackett tugged at his bottom lip for a moment. "We'll be working with the locals, of course. Sergeant Hughes and a couple of uniformed types."

"Thought this was basically an open-and-shut case," said Daily. She glanced at Brackett, but there was no kindness in her eyes.

"That's why Carnes dragged me away last night. We've a major complication that involves Dennis Profitt. Might not be related to the first case. Might be a coincidence, though I don't believe in coincidences."

"Stop beating around the bush," snapped Daily.

"Profitt's wife was found dead in their sauna yesterday, sometime after the robot went berserk. Dead in a locked room. Probably of natural causes, but the police were called in and did spend some time investigating. We'll meet with the officers involved with that."

"Great," said Daily. "Now I understand what Carnes was saying. We're not to look too hard at this. Profitt kills his wife and we're to whitewash it."

Brackett looked at her. "I don't remember anything like that being discussed."

"Profitt owns that town. Hell, he owns the whole planet. You think that they're going to allow us to arrest him for killing her."

"First," said Brackett, "we don't know that he killed her. And second, I would think that the planetary officials, not to mention a hundred different corporations and other worlds' governments, would be pleased to have Profitt arrested. Means that they could cease paying him royalties. All that money would drop into their corporate coffers."

"Right," said Daily.

"Jesus," said Tate. "This could be the story of the century."

Brackett took a deep breath and shook his head. "This is not the story of the century. It could be an accidental death. Nothing more. According to this Hughes, there was no sign of foul play. It looks as if she locked herself in the sauna and then was overcome by the heat."

"Right," said Daily.

There was a bong and then a bump. The intercom of the shuttle came alive. "We've entered the planet's atmosphere. We anticipate touchdown in twenty-two minutes."

"That doesn't give us much time," said Brackett. "I hoped that we could use the up-link and get a good briefing on this Profitt character."

"I'd like to see the police reports," said Daily.

"Up-link to the police facility on the planet's surface is available."

"Maybe we just wait and go in cold," said Obo.

Brackett started to shake his head and then stopped. "Maybe Obo is right." He closed his eyes for a moment and then opened them, looking at Daily. "Let's do this. Let's go in to study the robot problem and take on the second case as an aside. Tread carefully."

"Great," said Daily.

"Sergeant Jennifer seem on edge," said Obo.

"Yeah. Well, ask the loot about that," she said.

"I'd hoped that we could avoid a confrontation until we had an opportunity to discuss it as two intelligent individuals. Just so you know, Carnes dragged me from the Cup and Hole up to his office for a strategy session. He doesn't want to find himself pounding a beat near galactic center if we happen to screw up and irritate the great man."

"Sure."

"We'll be touching down in ten minutes," announced the shuttle commander. "Please prepare for landing."

"Thought it was getting a little warm in here," said Tate, not referring to the internal cabin temperature.

The shuttle rolled to a stop short of the main terminal building and away from the security devices set up for the commercial space fleet. The shuttle ways, buses, and the air-conditioning were set up to keep paying passengers happy and comfortable.

The 107th's shuttle was directed to a parking space beneath the terminal. There was a cinder-block wall in front of it, and a concrete wall to the right, creating a nice, shady place to park the shuttle. A yellow tug raced across the tarmac and pulled up close. Two coveralled people jumped from it and plugged the external power into the shuttle.

Brackett stood and stretched. "Guess it's time that we got to work." He walked toward the front of the shuttle, ducked through the main hatch, and stood, waiting for a crew member to open the outside hatch.

The hatch cycled automatically on command from the cockpit, and swung up and out of the way. As the steps dropped down, a taste of the hot and humid atmosphere boiled up, into the shuttle.

"Damn. Another tropical planet," said Tate. "I hate the heat and humidity."

Brackett stepped down to the concrete. The air tasted metallic and stunk of jet fuel. There were old-fashioned jet airliners sitting on the ground. One had its engines running, the roar of them partially lost in the distance. Clouds of black smoke poured from the rear.

"Thought there'd be a delegation here to meet us," said Brackett.

Then, as if to prove him right, a man rushed from a red painted door. Two uniformed officers followed him. When he saw Brackett and his crew, he slowed to a walk.

Approaching, he asked, "Lieutenant Brackett?"

"Right. With Sergeant Daily, Officer Obo, and a journalist who has promised that everything for the moment is off the record."

"Great," said the man. "I'm Hughes with Officers OBrien and Ryan."

Brackett ran a hand through his hair and said, "I know what you're thinking. We're going to screw up your investigation. We're going to take over, grab any credit we can, and hang you out if things don't go right. We're just the glory boys down from orbit to save the local yokels."

Hughes hesitated for just a second and then said, "I wasn't thinking in terms that good."

Daily asked, "Is there someplace else we could talk? I'm sweating through my clothes."

"In the car," said Hughes. "I've got transportation laid on, accommodations have been arranged, and we can get a complete briefing on the activities, including the current status of the investigation."

"I must say," said Brackett, "I'm a little surprised by your attitude. Pleased, but surprised."

"I've been told to give you everything you want and to make it clear that it's your investigation. If you succeed and Mr. Profitt is pleased, there'll be rewards for all of us. You fail and you go down in flames by yourself, which is fine with me," said Hughes.

They started for the red door. Ryan hitchhiked a thumb over his shoulder. "That a Tau?"

"Yes," said Obo. "I am tall."

"Christ," said Ryan.

Hughes led them through the terminal, avoiding customs, mandatory medical, and currency exchange where shuttleport taxes were to be paid. He kept them in the basement, walking down a cinder-block corridor that was brightly lighted but that seemed to have no doors and no end.

Finally they reached another red door that Hughes opened with a key. They stepped out into the blinding sunlight of the exterior parking lot. Hughes, OBrien, and Ryan all had dark glasses. None of Brackett's team did. No one had warned them that the sun was three times Earth normal. Brackett put a hand over his eyes. Daily closed hers and Tate tried to see. Only Obo didn't mind the sunlight. Tau Ceti, as seen from his planet, was brighter than this and his eyes were able to adjust to the brightness.

"Sorry," said Hughes. "Thought you knew. If you'll wait here, I'll go get the car. Windows are tinted." He hurried across the road and walked down into the parking lot.

Daily moved close to Brackett and lowered her voice. "He did that on purpose."

"Of course. He's telling us that this is his home turf. We're the interlopers."

"Asshole," said Daily.

"Of course," agreed Brackett.

The ground car arrived. It was a big vehicle, looking more like a hovercraft with seating for twelve than it did a personal car.

"After you," said OBrien. She stood with her hands on her hips.

Daily climbed up the two steps, being careful of her short skirt, entered, and dropped onto the couch that was up against the bulkhead. Obo was next. His weight caused the hovercraft to dip slightly. There was a sudden whir as the engines tried to compensate for him.

"Fucking aliens," said Ryan.

Brackett shot him a glance but didn't say anything. Not until he had a better feel for the chain of command. He assumed that Ryan was under Hughes, but until he knew for sure, he wasn't going to say a thing. Sometimes the locals did that. Stuck a high-ranking official in with the troops to get a better feel for the Star Cops. A misplaced word at the wrong time and months of hard work could crash down.

Once they were inside, with the hatch closed, Hughes turned around, an arm up on the pilot's seat back. "What do you want to do first?"

"I would imagine," said Brackett, "that we should check in with your chief and let him establish the ground rules. Then check the computer files before we see the crime scene."

"Okay," said Hughes. "I thought you'd want to head over to the Star Rest right away. Get right to work."

"There something here that you're not telling us?" asked Brackett.

"Nope. I'm just here to help."

Daily broke in. "I thought that was supposed to be our line."

"Yeah," said Hughes. "That's what's got me scared."

7 | It Was in the Cards

Ambassador Sumner Gleason left the penthouse just before dawn, about an hour before the last of the police officials had cleared out. He took the high-speed elevator to the ground floor, stepped into the main lobby, and watched as the hotel staff swarmed around him supposedly because he was a high-ranking official but in reality trying to learn what was going on in the penthouse.

Gleason moved through the lobby, trying not to look right or left because the newsies and the vidjournalists had descended like the vultures when something died. They shouted questions at him, turned their bright lights on him, and followed him as he moved to the double doors that led to the outside.

Only a couple of them followed him outside, still shouting their questions. He knew that if he answered anything now, as he was about to escape them, the rest would note it and they'd hound him forever. The best action was not to speak to them unless it was at a formal press conference, or just after he came from the main meeting or scene of the action. If he spoke as he tried to leave, they'd surround his car, they'd pound on the windows, and they'd run down the street following him, trying for that one last quote, that one bit of unique and therefore exclusive tape.

His car was parked on the street, a privilege reserved for those with rank. Citizens had to have their cars, if they could afford to own one, off the streets, so that the sanitation crews could sweep through without obstruction.

As he darted across the street, dodging a single hover vehicle, he left the reporters behind. They stood on the curb, still shouting at him, but a couple had turned off their cameras. Now would be the perfect time to screw a couple of them. If he wanted. But the long-term result would be a pack of the jackals after him for all time.

Safe in his car, he slumped back, felt the sweat bead and drip, and took a deep breath. He glanced to the right, but the reporters had retreated to the hotel lobby where there was air-conditioning and the opportunity to ambush someone else who'd just come from the penthouse.

He started the car, felt it shift as it came up off the ground, hovering on a cushion of air. He let it idle and reached over to turn on the radio, sliding through the all-music, all-commercial, all-talk to the all-news. The lead story, repeated every five minutes by a breathless voice that could have been either male or female, was that something involving Dennis Profitt had happened at the Star Rest Imperium Hotel, but officials weren't commenting.

Gleason slipped into gear and turned out onto the street without looking at the traffic. It was up to the others to avoid him. His was an official vehicle.

He drove through the morning streets without a destination. His thoughts were back in Profitt's penthouse, and on the body of the young wife. So young and so beautiful to be dead. It was a crime that she was dead. Profitt should be blamed, even if it was only his life-style that was guilty.

Gleason turned down a side street, saw that no one was following him, turned again, and pulled over to the curb. There was a danger, leaving his official car here, but the police, the politicians, and even the vidjournalists had been trained to ignore it. There were times that a man needed his privacy. A man had needs that had to be serviced, and someone investigating those regions found himself shipped off-planet rapidly. Often in a craft that just didn't have the capability to make it to the next port.

Gleason shut down his car, exited, and then stretched in the early morning light. He locked the car and then turned, making sure that there was no one watching him. He walked to the curb and then strolled along the sidewalk, detouring around a puddle of something mysterious and sticky, under a huge tree that dropped its purple fruit on the ground around it, and past a barking dog that looked more friendly than dangerous.

He reached a second car. This was an older model with faded paint, a rock-pitted windshield that had some of the tint peeling, and a bent license plate that obscured some of the numbers. Gleason used his key and climbed in.

A moment later, he had it started, glanced at the flow of traffic, or rather the lack of it, and pulled out. He drove into a poorer part of the city. One where there were hotels that catered to a crowd that didn't want the room for the night, where there were rooming houses that didn't require references, and where the people ignored those around them.

Gleason parked his car behind another that could have been its twin. He got out, glanced right and left, and hurried across the street, to a sidewalk that was cracked in a hundred places. He finally entered the miniature yard of an old rooming house. He used the fire escape to climb to the second floor, slipped down a hallway that smelled of stale beer, urine, and vomit, and stopped at a door that was scratched badly, dented in two places, but was as solid as brick. He used a key, opened the door, and entered the small apartment.

It was a single room with a bath off to the right. The bed, a four-poster, stood next to the wall and away from the single window. The tint had cracked in a couple of places and peeled in a few others. It created a patchwork on the threadbare carpet. A wardrobe stood next to the window and there was a dresser beside it, holding framed pictures.

He picked up one of them and looked at the woman in it. Tall, blond, in a low-cut dress that displayed her two main attributes to the satisfaction of all those interested. A pretty woman who knew how to manipulate the men who came to hear her sing sad songs at one of the four clubs that catered to the lonely miners, traders, salesmen, and adventurers.

The wardrobe held her clothes, along with those for a man. The dresser contained more of her things. She'd bought the bed at an auction, and stayed in the rooming house because the rent was cheap. She told those who asked that she was saving so that she could return to Vega in style. It made a good story.

Gleason went into the bathroom and splashed water on his face. He looked at himself in the cracked mirror and then dried himself on a threadbare towel. Then, stripping off his coat and tie, he lay down on the bed, his eyes on the window where the sun was beginning to blaze. He would be left alone there. No one would come there looking either for him, or for Lana. Not for several hours. If at all.

Although Profitt had been awake all night, and although his wife died fifteen or twenty hours earlier, Profitt appeared in his office almost on time. Fortunately, he hadn't had to leave the hotel to get to the office, nor had he had to use the main elevators. Having money meant he could afford to install a private elevator that could reach the penthouse, the landing zone on the roof, the lobby, or the seventy-first through eighty-ninth levels where he had his office complex.

He stepped out of the elevator, and found himself facing his private secretary, Rachel de vo Willom, a slightly reptilian-looking woman from the marsh world of Fomalhaut Three. Their ancestors, at some point, had to have been human because their genetic makeup was close enough to the human to allow some interbreeding, and they were amazingly human-looking, except for the leathery skin and lack of hair.

"I have taken the liberty of canceling all your morning appointments," she said, looking at him. "I can reschedule them for later in the week. I have done nothing about the afternoon appointments yet."

Profitt stopped and looked at her. Tall and skinny. Her eyes were oval-shaped and very dark, nearly black. Sometimes she wore a wig of long black hair, sometimes a short one of blond hair, but most of the time, she wore no wig. Just her bald head gleaming in the office lights.

The only thing that bothered Profitt was her fingers. They were much longer than a human's, skinnier, looking almost like tentacles, and then a short, fat opposing thumb.

Her legs looked human but it seemed that she was always wearing soft leather boots that molded themselves to her. Her feet were small, almost dainty, and Profitt knew that she had no toes.

"In my office," said Profitt. He pointed at a male aide and another secretary who were standing to the side. "All in my office." He then walked on through ignoring the dozens of others who had questions for him.

As soon as the door was closed, he said, "Rachel, I'll want all appointments for the next two days rescheduled. Bump them with kindness but remember, they want to meet with me, so don't create extra work for yourself."

"Yes, sir."

He looked at the male aide, Pete Davies, a thin, angular man with rapidly thinning hair and a nonexistent beard. He was fussy, demanded things done his way. He sat with a minicomputer near him and a pad of paper on his lap.

"Pete, I want you to meet with the press and tell them nothing. We'll draft a statement later and that'll be the final response we'll have on it. We'll let the police handle everything."

"Yes, sir. Let me say that we're all devastated by the events. Crushed."

"Thank you."

He looked at the last person, a young woman who'd joined his staff only months earlier, but because of her youth and her looks, she'd moved from the steno pool, to the typing pool, to Profitt's private secretarial staff. Linda Thoresson. She opted for the most revealing clothing she could find. Clinging, short, flimsy. She had long brown hair with bangs that brushed her blue eyes.

"Linda, I want you to make the arrangements for the funeral. Select the clothes for burial . . ."

"Burial or cremation?"

Profitt was quiet for a moment and then said, "I think there will be a viewing and then, I think, cremation, in keeping with the traditions of Earth. I think that her family would want it that way."

"Yes, sir. I'll get on it."

"Rachel, I don't want to see anyone but my priest, Sumner Gleason, or Richard Spelman."

"Yes, sir."

"That's all I have," said Profitt. "You have your jobs. Let's get to them."

Rachel and Pete left immediately, but Linda stayed behind. As Rachel closed the door on her way out, Linda set her pad on the chair and moved toward Profitt. She wrapped her arms around him and said, "I'm so sorry."

Profitt held her close, feeling her body against his, aware that she was definitely female. "Thank you."

"If there is anything that I can do, anything at all, please let me know."

A dozen thoughts flashed through his mind but he didn't mention any of them. Instead he gently disengaged himself. He walked around and sat behind his desk. It dwarfed him, making him look like the kid sitting behind his father's desk. The wall of books behind him, carefully selected for the colors of the dust jackets, reached from the floor to the ceiling twelve feet above him. There were thousands of books, but none of them had been read by Profitt or anyone else on his staff.

Linda walked around and leaned against the edge of his desk. She crossed her ankles and folded her arms under her breasts. Looking down at Profitt, she asked, "Are you going to be all right?"

"It was those damned health freaks. Tony and William. They had her in the pool swimming laps in heat that could kill a bull elephant. That's what did it."

"Want me to have them fired?"

Profitt steepled his fingers under his chin. Closing his eyes, he said, "No. Not yet."

"Anything else?" she asked.

Profitt opened his eyes and turned in his chair so that he was facing her. He reached out and cupped the back of her leg, running his hand up, under the hem of her skirt. She was wearing stockings and not panty hose and that surprised him. He rubbed the soft inner skin of her thigh.

She closed her eyes, tilted her head back, and moaned low in her throat. "That feels so good."

Profitt let his fingers linger on the silky flesh of her upper thigh. For just a moment a picture of his dead wife lying in the sauna flashed in his mind, but then it was replaced with a picture of Linda, totally nude, standing in front of him. He liked the image.

He pulled at her and she moved away from the desk, standing at the side of his chair. She made no move to pull down the hem of her skirt so that he could study her legs, the tops of her stockings, and the tanned, taut skin of her inner thighs.

There was a buzz then. Profitt ignored it for a moment and then reached out, touching a button on his desk. "Father Robert is here," Rachel announced.

"Thank you," he told Rachel but kept his hand under Linda's skirt. Letting go of the button on the intercom, he said to Linda, "I'll expect you to be at the penthouse this afternoon around two."

"I'll be there earlier to get things ready for Janet's funeral."

"Okay."

She stepped closer, bent, and kissed him quickly on the cheek. Then, tugging at her skirt, she walked to the door. "Later."

Profitt took a moment to compose himself. When she turned the full power of her personality, her body, her intelligence on him, it was almost too much to resist. He took a handkerchief from his pocket and patted at the sweat beaded on his forehead and upper lip.

A moment later the door opened and Father Robert entered.

He was almost a stereotypical priest. Tall and slim with just the hint of an accent when he spoke. His black hair was shot through with gray. He had piercing blue eyes and a personality that was nearly as arresting as Linda's.

"I am sorry, my son, that we meet under these circumstances."

"Thank you, Father."

"Shall we pray?"

"Yes."

Linda stopped in the outer office and watched as the priest entered Profitt's office. As the door closed, she left, walking down a narrow hallway to her own office that was about one-sixth the size of her boss's. She sat behind her small desk and opened the bottom drawer, taking out what looked to be a deck of playing cards. Standing, she stepped to the door, locked it, a privilege available to only the most trusted of the employees, and then moved to the window.

Her view was one of the best, letting her look down on the city, and beyond it to the shallow sea that reached out into the deeper oceans half a hundred klicks farther. There were only a few clouds in the sky, the sun beating down on the city, turning it a brilliant white.

She opened the cards, pulled a small wire from it, pointed it at the window, and then said, "I have secured my position with Profitt. Meeting after two this afternoon."

She closed the miniature transmitter with its coded burst transmission that was almost impossible to detect, monitor, or jam. The receiver was four klicks away and disguised as a billboard that announced one of Profitt's newest enterprises.

Finished, she put the cards back in her desk, and then sat down again. There was nothing for her to do until two in the afternoon.

8 | To Protect and to Serve

Brackett wasn't used to sitting in a warm room, a humid room, and pawing through stacks of paper that weren't printouts. Computer time was so valuable on the planet's surface that the police had very little access to it. They kept their files on paper and cards and stuck in rows upon rows of file cabinets that filled several rooms. It was the way things had been done decades earlier on Earth.

Of course, on the frontier worlds, it was to be expected.

Daily, looking as if she were about to melt, slumped over the table, tried to push her sweat-damp hair from her eyes, and said, "Can't we take a break?"

Brackett stopped and looked at her and then at Obo who stood near the window, looking out onto the street. He'd been there almost from the moment they'd entered the tiny office. He was trying, in his way, to get a feel for the planet.

"What did the service records, the maintenance data, and the diagnostic examination show?"

Without looking up, Daily said, "Service and maintenance records are up-to-date and certified. The diagnostic showed that the robot had not malfunctioned."

"Then it just attacked the man and threw him down the elevator shaft for no reason."

Now she sat up and looked right at Brackett. "No. I told you before. It did not malfunction."

"Which means it was doing its job," said Brackett sarcastically. Then, suddenly, he added, "Oh. Oh. We got anything on that . . . O'Shaughnessy?"

"Nothing here," said Daily.

"Okay," said Brackett, wiping the sweat from his face. "Let's take a few minutes off. I'm going to talk to Hughes and see what he has."

"Air-conditioning," said Daily. "That's what I need."

Brackett stood up and then laughed. "That's the problem with the 107th. The environment is controlled all the time. Perfect weather all the time. Then we make planetfall, and everyone falls apart."

Obo turned from the window. "I am happy with the environment."

"Of course you are," said Daily.

"I'll be back in a few minutes. You two are free to do whatever you want until I return. Then I want to make a run over to the Star Rest."

"It have air-conditioning?" asked Daily.

"I'm sure it does."

"Then I'm ready."

Brackett left the small office, walked along a corridor that was dim and dirty and narrow. He reached a staircase and climbed to the next floor and then walked to Hughes's office. He knocked on the door even though it was open and he could see Hughes sitting behind his desk.

"Yes," said Hughes.

Brackett entered but didn't sit in the single chair set for visitors. The office was barely large enough for the desk, chair, and a bookcase that was empty. There was no window, no fan, and no circulation of air. Hughes didn't seem to be affected by the heat and humidity.

"Have a couple of questions for you."

Hughes dropped his pencil and pointed at the chair. "Have a seat."

Brackett sat down and said, "We've got everything we need on the robot, but we've nothing on the victim."

"Why would you want that? Robot went berserk, attacked and killed the man, and then returned to duty."

"That's it," said Brackett. "Everyone assumes a malfunctioning robot, but there is no evidence of that. Up-to-date maintenance records and the diagnostic suggest no malfunction. The only conclusion that can be drawn is that the robot was doing its job."

"O'Shaughnessy was a priest or minister or whatever they call themselves. A religious leader, dressed in the red robes of his sect."

"Did you check him out?"

"You want the file on it?" asked Hughes, sounding like Brackett were an annoying child.

"I'd appreciate anything that you could give me on this," said Brackett.

"Fine." Hughes turned and opened a desk drawer. He threw a file folder on his desktop. "This is our preliminary report. It gives everything we know about O'Shaughnessy."

Brackett leaned forward to take it.

"Nothing here out of the ordinary," said Hughes.

"You investigate him at all? There been people around to protest his death at the mechanical hands of a berserk robot? Family? Fellows of this religious sect?"

"You can see what we've got," said Hughes, pushing the folder forward.

Brackett took the folder and opened it. On top was an eight-by-ten full-color photograph of the body as it looked once it had plunged down the ninety-six stories. It looked as if they could have blotted it up with a sponge. Not much that was recognizable as a human body.

Brackett paid no attention to it. He'd seen worse. Besides, a photograph, no matter how graphic, couldn't make him sick. He'd seen the worst that the vidproducers could invent and the photo was tame by those standards.

There were no photos of the man before his untimely and grisly demise. Brackett scanned the report and then asked, "You got a picture of him before his death?"

"We've requested that from the central files but it hasn't come in yet."

"Computer link?"

"Time is precious. No need to waste it on a routine matter," said Hughes.

"Mind if I take this?"

"Make sure that I get it back."

Brackett stood up and said, "You know, we're here to help you."

"Right. And the check is in the mail."

"Sometimes the check is," said Brackett. "Thanks for your help." He walked out and headed back to the small office they were using.

There, he found that Daily hadn't moved. She was still seated at the table, her head down. Obo was still watching the world outside the building swirl around.

"Obo," said Brackett, holding out the folder, "I want you to get this transmitted up to the precinct and then have them tap into the planetary computer system and get us a current photo of the victim. Also, anything they have on him and anything they have on this sect." Brackett sifted through the folder. "This Hare O'Shaughnessy splinter sect."

"I do that right now this very minute." Obo took the folder, sat down, and then opened the briefcase that held their up-link equipment.

"What's going on?" asked Daily without lifting her head.

"We have now eliminated the routine. We begin to look at the extraordinary . . . or, I suppose, the ordinary. That is, that the robot was doing its duty."

When Brackett left his office, Hughes picked up his pencil again, studied it as if it contained all the answers to all the questions in the universe, and then threw it at the wall as hard as he could. It hit point first and shattered, the splinters flying in a satisfactory explosion of wood and lead. Then, with the anger burned away, he stood and walked out.

He found both OBrien and Ryan sitting in the squad room,

both reading reports that had been filed the night before by the investigating officers and the lab technicians who had arrived after they had determined that Mrs. Profitt was definitely dead.

Pulling out a chair and spinning it around so that he could straddle it, Hughes sat down. He propped his chin on his arm that was across the back of the chair. "What you got there?"

OBrien waved her paper at him like it was a flag of surrender and said, "Lab says that it can find no evidence to reject Profitt's claim that he broke the window to enter the sauna. Or that once locked from the inside, there was no way to enter it without someone on the inside opening the door."

"Shit."

"Which is not to say," OBrien added hastily, "that Profitt is telling the truth. Only that there is no evidence that he is not telling the truth."

"Let's talk in circles some more," said Hughes sarcastically.

"Hey," said OBrien.

"Sorry. I've just had a meeting with that Space Cop. Pissed me off."

"Anyway," said OBrien, ignoring that and the apology, "it means that we don't know what happened."

"Medical examiner," said Ryan, taking over, "said that he could see no evidence of foul play visible on her body. No wounds, no signs of any type of heavy metal poisoning, and no signs of any disease that would cause her death. But he added that the autopsy might reveal something that wasn't immediately visible."

"When are we to get the results?"

Ryan grinned broadly. "Since this was Mrs. Profitt, and because there was political influence, as well as the visit by the Star Cops, the autopsy has been completed."

"Shit! One of us should have attended."

"Why?" asked OBrien, looking slightly green at the thought.

"So that if we end up in court we can say that we were there. So that we could ask questions that the medical examiner or the coroner might not have thought of to ask. So that we could make suggestions based on our observations at the scene of the crime."

"If a crime has been committed," said Ryan, grinning slyly.

"Right," agreed Hughes. But he was thinking of the tiny crimson tear at the corner of her eye that might have had great significance and which, as the body was prepared for the post, might have been washed away in the normal course of events. Such a tiny thing that could have been destroyed by throwing a towel over her face, or rubbed away as she was stuffed into a rubber body bag. A trace of evidence that might have led to something greater, if the technicians had left it right where it had appeared.

"And?" asked Hughes.

"We have a murder!" said Ryan as if telling Hughes that he was the jackpot winner.

"Shit!"

"What?" said OBrien.

Hughes looked at her and decided that she could be forgiven her naiveté. The young ones and the rookies often saw murders as the way to shine. Solve the case and win approval and promotion. But murders, real whodunits, were almost impossible to solve because the range of suspects was limited and when they were eliminated, there was no place to go.

Suspects in this case were Profitt, Klaus, and no one else. No one had been in the penthouse at the time. And the locked door, if it had been locked, seemed to eliminate both of them, unless they were in collusion. Of course, Profitt had the money to buy just about anything he wanted.

Looking at OBrien, Hughes asked, "You think the husband did it?"

OBrien looked at her desktop, at the stack of papers there, including her report on her interview with Profitt. She touched it as if to reassure herself that it was real.

"He was coming on to me," she said.

"Let's be professional," said Hughes. "Tell me your reactions in a professional sense."

"He studied my chest and my legs as we talked. He moved

into my space, reaching out to touch my hand and arm as we discussed the death of his wife. It struck me that someone might have broken a valuable vase that he owned. One that couldn't be exactly replaced, but one that had thousands of variations still available."

"That make him a murderer?" asked Hughes.

"No. My gut reaction is that he didn't do it. Her death is an inconvenience to him, but hell, he didn't have to kill her to get rid of her."

Ryan broke in. "There was a prenuptial agreement that gave her a couple of mil in the event of a divorce. And she had a separate bank account with just under two million in it. But Profitt's got so much money he could have given her half and never felt it."

"So what you're saying is that we've a murder with no motive."

OBrien nodded. "That's it, Tom."

Hughes sat up and rubbed his chin slowly. He glanced at Ryan. "You haven't mentioned the method?"

"You might call it both sophisticated and clumsy at once."

"Meaning?"

"A sharpened wire shoved up into the brain through the corner of the eye. Causing a hemorrhage that suppressed the brain function killing the victim."

"Fairly sophisticated."

"Except for the telltale traces it leaves, including that drop of blood at the eye. A sophisticated killer would have wiped it away. That gave the whole plan away much too easily," said Ryan.

Hughes dropped his chin back to his arm on the rear of the chair. "That leads to one final question. Shoving a needle or wire into someone's eye is not the easiest thing in the universe. Since there was no external evidence of damage, we can assume that she didn't struggle. Why is that? Any sign of drugs in the body? Signs that she had been restrained?"

"Sorry, Tom," said Ryan. "The only thing the coroner found was the track of the needle. Straight into the brain. No sign that she resisted it at all and no signs of drugs in her system, other than a small amount of alcohol suggesting she'd had wine with lunch, and no sign of restraint."

"So we've got ourselves a real whodunit?"

"The Star Cops are looking into a robot that went crazy," said OBrien. "We wrap this up and they're going to look bad."

Hughes studied her for a moment. "Who did it?" he asked.

"What do you mean?"

"Who killed her?"

"Had to be Profitt. Either he did it. Or had Klaus do it."

"You just told me that your gut reaction was that he didn't do it."

"Yeah. But there is no one else to have done it."

"Okay," said Hughes patiently. "How?"

"Used a wire or a needle . . ."

"No," said Hughes. "I mean, how did he kill her and leave her in the locked room and then get out."

That stopped her for a moment but Ryan spoke up. "We've only their word that they had to break in. They're lying."

"Prove it," said Hughes.

Ryan understood the demand immediately. He said, "We can't. Yet."

Hughes stood up and looked down at the two officers. "You can design all the theories that you want but unless you can prove it, you've got nothing. And with a man like Profitt, you'd better have it nailed down six ways from Sunday or his attorney's going to dance rings around you."

"So he gets away with it," said OBrien.

Hughes shook his head and said, "You tell me that your gut tells you he didn't do it, but you're ready to nail him for it anyway."

"He had to do it."

"I would agree. There is no one else." And then he thought of the ambassador standing over the body when he had returned from the living room. But the ambassador hadn't been in the sauna when Profitt had broken in. Neither Klaus nor Profitt had mentioned him in their stories and had the ambassador been there, both would have mentioned him. One more witness to their version of events.

"So what do we do?" asked OBrien.

"We do what all cops have done throughout all of history. We keep our eyes and ears open and we wait for Profitt to make the one mistake that will give him away."

"Then you think he's guilty."

"There's no one else."

Profitt was working at his desk, or, rather, was pretending to work at his desk. His mind was elsewhere and although he was shuffling the papers that Rachel had given him, he had no clue about what was on the papers.

There was a tap at his door, which opened and then Davies stuck his head in. "You have a moment, sir?"

Profitt rocked back in his chair, pinched the bridge of his nose, and said, "Yeah. What do you have?"

"We picked up another burst transmission from here. We were waiting for it this time and we've got a location. We know where it came from."

Profitt waved Davies forward and pointed to one of the visitor's chairs. Davies dropped into it gratefully.

"How bad is it?" asked Profitt.

"We haven't been able to decode it yet, but we've got people working on it. We figure, based simply on the length of the burst, and the fact it was on a single frequency, that there wasn't much information contained in it. Certainly nothing that is going to hurt us in the long run."

Profitt took a deep breath and for a moment thought of everything that was going on around him. His wife was dead, there were police officers crawling over everything in search of answers, and now this.

"You have a location?"

"Yes, sir. And I think we've got their antenna spotted. We can begin low-level jamming. They shouldn't notice that until they realize they're getting no new reports."

"Good."

"Yes, sir. That's the good news. I'm afraid the rest of it isn't going to be that good."

"Might as well give it to me straight."

"Yes, sir. From the looks of things, it seems that Linda Thoresson is responsible for the transmission."

"Shit."

Davies rubbed his face, as if suddenly under a great deal of stress. Looking at the floor so that he could avoid Profitt's stare, he said, "I know that she's one of your favorites. You've brought her up fast, but the transmission came from her office."

"Which doesn't mean that she was responsible for it," said Profitt.

"No, sir, but I'd bet she is. She's the newest member of the inner circle here. And the trouble didn't start until she joined us."

Profitt rubbed his forehead as if he'd just gotten a headache from eating ice cream too fast. "I suppose that I'll have to fire her."

"Or limit her access to confidential information."

"I don't like being betrayed," said Profitt. "I brought her up, out of the typing pool, because she was bright and efficient and clever. This is my reward."

"Before you move," said Davies, "let's make sure that she is responsible. We wouldn't want to accuse someone unfairly."

Profitt waved a hand. "Oh, I have no doubt about it. Everything fits perfectly now."

"Yes, sir." Davies rose to leave.

Profitt stopped him. "Thanks for your work on this. I appreciate the effort."

"Thank you, sir."

9 | A Day in the Life

Linda Thoresson entered the penthouse carefully and quietly, almost as if she were afraid that she would wake the dead, though the body had been removed hours earlier. She used the key that she had collected from Rachel and then closed the door. She walked to the stairs that led up to the main level of the apartment but didn't climb them. For a moment she felt like a criminal who was invading a home to rob it.

The foyer was impressive. A wide expanse of tile that was large enough to house a yacht. Twenty feet to the right was a wall of mirror, partially masked by a narrow table that held fresh-cut, imported flowers—not from another area of the planet, but from another solar system.

Thoresson looked at herself in the mirror and then moved closer. She decided, as she had on a thousand other occasions when she'd been privileged to see herself in a full-length mirror, that she was quite a package. A shape that stopped men on the street, legs that were long and curvaceous, and a face that was lean and angular, but still beautiful. These were her main weapons and she used them to her full advantage.

Turning away from the mirror, she climbed the wide, curving stairway. A chandelier of cut glass hung over it. The light shattered and sparkled and twinkled, dancing around the foyer, making it seem alive.

She stopped at the top of the stairs, amazed, as always, by the sight. So much room. So much space, all for one man. It seemed almost obscene.

She turned and walked down a hallway and came to the dressing room that had belonged to Janet Profitt. It was as large as the master bedroom in many of the biggest houses in the city. There were racks of clothes, drawers filled with clothes, boxes of shoes, and cupboards of sweaters. Near the door was a series of buttons but Thoresson didn't know what any of them did. She'd never been privileged to see the dressing room before.

She entered, walked to the drawers, and pulled one open. It was filled with stockings of all types. Textured, transparent, panty hose, knee-high, and thigh-high. Every type of stocking, sock, or hose that a woman could ever want to put on her leg was in the drawer.

Others held underwear, panties and bras and half slips and tap pants and teddies. One drawer held only things that were red. Another had black and a third had white. There were lacy clothes, solid clothes, and see-through clothes. More undergarments than a single woman could wear in her entire life even if she never wore the same thing twice.

Turning slowly, she looked at the sweaters. Bulky and sleeveless and pullover. Reds and greens and browns and blacks. Wool sweaters and synthetics. Expensive sweaters and cheap ones. Every kind of sweater imaginable.

Thoresson stood in the dressing room and thought that most of the stores she'd seen didn't have the selection available to Janet Profitt. If she wanted to "shop" but didn't want to leave the penthouse, she could come to this room and wander the aisles between the racks and drawers and search for something interesting to wear.

She retreated to the front and touched one of the buttons. A long rack of dresses began to circulate looking like the huge arrangements that dry cleaners used. It circulated the dresses so that Janet Profitt wouldn't have to walk among them.

And the range of dresses was appalling. Long ones in black or silk or with sequins. Short ones in bright colors. Some with long sleeves and some with short and some with no sleeves at all. There were dresses to show off her legs, her shoulders, her back, or her breasts. There was one that looked like a series of leather straps that might have concealed her nipples and her pubic hair but it would be a close call.

Thoresson lifted her thumb from the button, touched another, and the parade of garments stopped. She reached out and touched one of them. A filmy thing that was as light as a cloud. Thoresson shook her head. She'd never seen such a variety in her life. She started them moving again, watching as they drifted by her.

Speaking out loud, to herself, she said, "Something conservative." Though she didn't know why. Janet Profitt certainly wouldn't care. For some reason the phrase "live hard, die young, and leave a good-looking corpse" popped into her mind.

Still, conservative was the way to go. Janet Profitt would not care what she looked like, but her husband probably would. He'd want people to remember his wife as an intelligent, beautiful woman and not a sleazy bimbo.

The dresses were making their second circuit when Thoresson heard someone calling. She stopped the parade and stepped into the hallway. "Hello?"

A shape appeared at the far end of the corridor, coming toward her. Thoresson yelled "Hello" again and then recognized Rachel. "Oh, hi," she said. "I was just trying to decide which dress to pick for Janet's funeral."

Rachel didn't say anything. She moved closer and then stopped.

"Did Dennis send you to help?"

"You're very chummy with Mr. Profitt, aren't you?" said Rachel, her voice sounding a little strange, as if it were rusty from long disuse.

Thoresson shrugged and turned, moving back into the dressing room. She started the dresses moving again and waited until Rachel joined her. Then she asked, "Do you think we should pick out underwear too, or will anyone care?"

Rachel watched the parade for a moment and then turned to

face Thoresson. Without a word, her right hand shot out and her long fingers closed around Thoresson's neck.

"Hey!" Thoresson shouted. She grabbed Rachel's wrist and tried to jerk her hand away, but couldn't make it budge. She tried to twist away, but Rachel's grip tightened, choking off the air. She tried to kick, but her foot missed the mark and she slipped. Rachel held on to her, lifting her from the floor. Claws seemed to penetrate her neck sending slivers of white-hot pain through her body.

With her free hand, she swung at Rachel, but it was a weak, halfhearted attempt. Blackness was beginning to descend. There were flashes of white and red as she clawed at the wrist. She tried to suck in air but the fingers around her throat were squeezing too tight. Her lungs burned and she was sick to her stomach because she couldn't breathe. The life was being squeezed from her.

Then, suddenly, the fingers slackened and she was able to get half a breath. She opened her eyes wide, focused for an instant on Rachel's reptilian face and then the dresses on the rack behind her.

Finally her world turned black and she wondered if someone had shut off the lights. It was the last thing that she thought. She didn't realize it when she died.

Profitt sat at his desk and couldn't wait for the time to pass. All he could think of was Linda up in the penthouse. He imagined her naked, standing in the hallway waiting for him. Or lying on the bed in the master bedroom, wearing a black teddy and stockings. Or dressed, completely dressed so that he'd have the fun of peeling her out of her clothes. His mind raced from vision to vision and he found his body responding to his thoughts.

And then he thought about what Davies had told him. Linda in her office, transmitting the corporate secrets to an unknown accomplice. It was a complete betrayal of everything that Profitt had worked for. Of course, he had so much. More than any other human in the universe so what did it matter if someone, if

Linda, was working to separate him from a little of that cash. Why should he even care?

The problem was that he didn't know now if Linda liked him for himself, or if she pretended to like him so that she could learn more about the operation.

A vision of her, naked, swam up in front of him. She was standing, one knee bent, a hand on her hip, a hand held out to him. Suddenly it didn't matter what the motivations were as long as she would stay near him.

Besides, he now knew what was happening. Business was one thing. He could understand the ruthless competitor in business. Ruthless, she might be, but now that he knew, he could negate the advantage. So, all things being equal, again, all he had to do was string her along. They could both gain from that.

He looked at the clock, watched it as it kept time, the seconds ticking off as slowly as the days passing. It seemed that eternity stretched in front of him. Two o'clock would never come. It receded into the distance to taunt him. Keep him on the edge but never allow him the release that he needed.

And then he realized that he didn't have to wait until two o'clock. That was an artificial time frame that he'd invented in his mind earlier when he'd been setting things up. Linda was in the penthouse now and he was free to join her if he wanted. Anticipation might be half the fun, but it was now past fun and approaching physical pain.

He stood up, made sure that his desk was locked, and walked across the office to open the door. He looked out at his private secretary and said, "I'll be upstairs in the penthouse. Same restrictions for callers."

"Certainly, sir."

Profitt retreated to the private elevator, entered, and said, "Penthouse."

A soft, feminine voice repeated the instruction. "Penthouse."

A moment later the doors opened, and Profitt stepped out. He glanced around but saw no evidence that Linda was there. Of course, she'd be in the rear of the penthouse, either searching for the clothes in which his wife would be buried, or she would be waiting for him to arrive.

He stopped at one of the four wet bars in the penthouse, poured himself a green label Beam's, and downed it in one quick gulp. He put the glass down on the bar, put the bottle back in the rack, and stepped around it.

For just an instant, he let his mind wander back to Davies and his announcement, worrying at it like a dog with a bone. Did it bother him that Linda might be an industrial spy? No. It didn't. It just made the game better, spicier. It was a new game now.

A flicker of movement near the hall caught his attention and he thought he saw Rachel running toward the back stairs. He moved forward but she'd gotten away.

"Rachel?"

There was no answer. He started toward the back stairs and then stopped. He turned, looked down the hall, and called, "Linda? You back there?"

For an instant he wasn't sure what to do. Check to see if it was Rachel or to see if Linda was in the rear of the penthouse. He stood still, took a step toward the stairs, and then another toward the hall. He looked like a toy thats directional gyro had failed.

Then, making up his mind, he moved rapidly across the carpet and touched the button on the flatscreen that would show him his office complex below. His office, naturally, was empty. In the outer reception area, Rachel sat at her desk. Of course, he couldn't tell if she had just run back down there. That was the thing about her. She never sweated. Her internal temperature would climb until she was forced to seek relief by bathing in cool water but she didn't sweat. Unless she was in the last stages of heat prostration, there was no way to tell if she had been exerting herself or not.

He leaned forward and said, "Rachel?"

She turned to face the camera. "Mr. Profitt."

"Were you just in the penthouse?"

"No, sir. I've been sitting right here since you left. Haven't moved. Why?"

"Nothing," said Profitt. He was sure that she was lying about it. He couldn't have been that wrong even if he hadn't gotten a good look. He shook himself. She hadn't had the time to get to her desk, even if the elevator had been waiting for her. Still . . .

He watched her for a moment. She stared at him, tried to smile, and then returned to her work. Profitt finally switched off.

"Linda?" he called then.

Again there was silence. He had the feeling of déjà vu. Was it only yesterday that he'd been searching for Janet and found her dead? It seemed as if it had been months, maybe years. He forgot what she looked like, how she sounded, what she was like. Her place had been taken by Linda Thoresson.

Profitt crossed to the hallway and looked down it. There was the whisper of one of the racks in the dressing room as it rotated. Linda had to be in there.

"Linda?" he said as he walked down the hall.

Still there was no response.

Anticipating her surprise, he slowed and then slipped over, against the wall. Like a thief, he slid along, his back to the wall, his head turned so that he was staring at the door. The noise from the rack was getting louder as he approached.

The body was lying facedown on the carpet. She was sprawled with her dress twisted around her hips so that he knew she was wearing red panties.

"That's not funny," he snapped, staring at her back, willing her to breathe. "Not funny at all."

He crouched then and reached out to touch her. There was no pulse at her throat and as he examined her, he saw that the skin was discolored, red and blue and black. He lifted her, turning her over, and got a good look at her face. The eyes were red, bright red, and her tongue was a bloody pulp protruding between her blue lips.

He sat back in shock, falling to his butt and reaching behind for the wall. "What in the hell happened?" He glanced at the door and hallway and thought about Rachel running from the penthouse.

"No. It couldn't be."

But everything told him that it was and it made no sense to him at all.

10 | It Was Déjà Vu All Over Again

Brackett was amazed that the hotel was as modern as it was. On the frontier worlds it was sometimes impossible to find a first-class hotel. The whims of the tourist were often ignored because it was too expensive to cater to those tastes, especially when the people with the money to afford the accommodations probably wouldn't be stopping off.

Of course, the difference was that the second-richest creature in the known universe was the main resident. He could afford anything he wanted and the people who ran the hotel wanted to please him.

Brackett let Obo open the door. The cold air rolled out and Daily stopped for a moment. Grinning broadly, she said, "Now this is more like it." She rushed in, stopping just beyond the door.

Brackett entered, scratched his head, and said, "Yes, this is nice."

"Maybe we could move over to this hotel," said Daily.

"I doubt that Carnes would appreciate it when we submitted the vouchers."

"I have money," she said.

"Not enough," said Brackett. He moved to the registration desk. He leaned on it, thinking that it looked as if it belonged in the middle of the twenty-first century. It was a combination of deep, solid wood and electronics that provided the customer with a view of what was happening.

"Yes, sir," said the clerk, a young man in a tailored suit, with neatly trimmed hair and the glowing skin of good health. "How may I help you?"

Brackett showed his badge and said, "We don't want to make trouble here, but we'd like to see the elevator shaft where the man was killed."

"Maintenance cleaned that all up," said the man.

"We have not completed our investigation," said Brackett.

"We were told that the police were finished and that we could clean it up. We needed to get the elevator back into service."

"I understand," said Brackett, "but I would like to see the shaft anyway. And then I want to see the point where the man was thrown in, and I'll like to see the robot that did it."

"Robot belongs to Mr. Profitt. You'll have to clear that with him."

"Then I'll just take a look at the shaft and the point where the man was thrown in."

"I'm going to have to get permission from the manager."

"You do that," said Brackett.

The man spun and hurried to the rear where the manager's office was located. Brackett turned, leaned an elbow on the counter, and watched Daily and Obo. Apparently most of the hotel staff and a majority of the hotel guests who were in the lobby had never seen a Tau before. They tried to study him without being obvious about it. Obo pretended that he didn't notice, but the attention was beginning to bother him. His eyes were blinking rapidly and he was rubbing at the peach fuzz on his arms.

The clerk returned and said, "The manager has asked that I escort you down to the basement and show you the shaft. If you'll come this way."

"Let's go," said Brackett.

Daily, who had dropped onto one of the couches and was letting the cold air wash over her, stood. Obo joined her, standing close to her as if he wanted her protection from all the people who were watching him.

They were led around the bank of elevators, to the rear where a service elevator, activated by a key, stood. The clerk opened it, entered, let the others join him, and then used his key to take them into the subbasement.

"There's not going to be anything to see. Our maintenance people cleaned the area thoroughly."

"Of course," said Brackett.

The doors popped open and the heat of machinery filled the elevator.

"Hell," said Daily, beginning to sweat before she stepped out.

The clerk led them across a dirty concrete floor. Boxes, broken equipment, furniture that had seen better days, and a rack of uniforms filled the area. A couple of dim bulbs created small pools of light. From the dark recesses came the scrambling of tiny claws.

Turning to look back, the clerk said, "The body, such as it was, was found in here."

"You see it?" asked Brackett.

"No. I wasn't on duty and if I had been, I wouldn't have wanted to see it. Quite a mess." He stood to one side of the elevator doors and used a key to open them.

"Where was the elevator?" asked Daily.

"I'm afraid that I don't understand."

"If the man was thrown down the shaft, wouldn't he have landed on top of the elevator?"

"Oh. It was above him, on one of the upper floors."

"Light," said Brackett, stepping forward.

The clerk moved back, rummaged around, and then turned on a flashlight.

Taking it, Brackett said, "Thanks." As he entered the shaft, searching the bottom with his light, he commented, "I would have thought that the elevators wouldn't run the entire way up and down the hotel."

"You'll notice that there are no cables, but a track in each of the corners. Elevator pulls itself up the shaft using electrical power. Slides back down. No long cables and no reason that it can't make the whole run."

Brackett crouched, shining the light into the corners, checking the floor, walls, and the rails. "Your maintenance people did one hell of a job."

There was a quiet buzzing and the clerk pulled a beeper from his pocket. "Yes?"

"Please inform the police officers that Mr. Profitt has requested assistance in the penthouse."

Daily said, "Now isn't that convenient? The man calls for us."

"We must hurry," said the clerk.

Brackett stood and said, "We're right behind you."

They hurried to the service elevator. As they entered, the clerk said, "I'm going to use the express speed. Please prepare for a rapid acceleration."

Daily moved into the corner and put her hands on the railings there as if to brace herself.

The doors closed and the clerk turned the key. The elevator seemed to leap upward. There was a clattering as the wheels gripped the rail. Pressure tried to force each of them to their knees.

Daily's face paled slightly and sweat was beaded on her upper lip. To take her mind off the rapid trip, she asked Brackett, "How are we going to handle this?"

"We're the first cops on the scene. Just like that," said Brackett.

The elevator slowed and then stopped, nearly knocking each of them from their feet. The door opened and the clerk said, "We'll need to walk up from here. Just two floors."

Without waiting, he rushed from the elevator, unlocked an access door, and took the steps two at a time. Brackett was right behind him.

They exited into a large, well-lighted hallway. At the far end was a massive double door. The clerk pointed and said, "Mr. Profitt's penthouse."

"Nice," said Brackett.

As they approached the door, it opened and a man appeared. The clerk looked back at the police officers and said, "That's Mr. Profitt."

Brackett, of course, had recognized him. The picture in the computer file hadn't been aged enough, but it was obvious who it was. He was immaculately attired in a light gray business suit and shoes so glossy that the shine was evident from forty feet away.

"She's dead," said Profitt.

Brackett said, "Who's dead?"

"Linda." He then spotted Obo. He studied the alien for a moment and asked, "What's that?"

"A police officer," said Brackett. "Where's the body?"

Profitt was now distracted. He glanced back, through the open door, and then back at Obo. "She's in the dressing salon."

"Where's that?" demanded Brackett.

"I don't want that creature in my house," said Profitt.

"I'm afraid that I don't give a shit what you want," said Brackett. "Officer Obo is with me."

He pushed past Profitt and into the entrance of the penthouse. The amount of space there, the roominess of it, immediately overwhelmed him. Living in what was a spaceship, even one as large as the 107th, meant that they had to use space wisely. There were very few wide-open areas. That was why they had gone to the expense of creating viewports. It let the people look out into the vastness of space and reduced the feelings of claustrophobia among the staff and crew.

But to have this much space seemed to be obscene. Not when people were crowded together in the ships. Not when his cabin on the ship would easily fit on the expanse of tile with room left over for another couple of cabins and most of the communications center.

And all the mirrors on the wall expanded the feeling of openness.

Daily stepped through, lifted a hand to her head, and said, "Oh, my God."

"Kind of leaps up and slaps you, doesn't it?"

Profitt had retreated from the door and now stood in front of the steps. "I won't allow that creature in my home."

"Mr. Profitt," said Brackett, his eyes darting from the mirrors to the stairs to the furnishings. "I don't believe the point is open for debate. Show us the body."

Profitt hesitated. It had been a long time since anyone had argued with him. It had been a long time since those receiving his orders hadn't leapt to obey them. For an instant he stood his ground and then turned.

They paraded up the stairs. Brackett found that he was holding on to the railing as if afraid that he would fall. Or be sucked into the vacuum that all the emptiness had to create.

They stopped at the head of the long hall. There was a quiet whisper of something mechanical moving. Profitt pointed and said, "The open door on the right."

Brackett looked at Daily and Obo, and then realized that the clerk had followed them into the penthouse. "Why don't you guard the door?" Brackett said to him. "No one comes in until we've finished."

"Certainly."

Turning his attention to Daily, he said, "Why don't you take Mr. Profitt into another room and get his statement?"

"Mr. Profitt?" said Daily, pointing into the cavernous living room.

As they moved off, Brackett said, "Let's go take a look at the body."

Without waiting for Obo to respond, Brackett hurried down the hall, scanning the carpeting in case something had been dropped. He found nothing. At the door, he stopped, but didn't enter.

With Obo, he examined the floor just outside the dressing salon. The carpeting was thick, showing the most recent traffic pattern, but the shapes in the carpet were too indistinct to be of use. Too many people had stepped onto the prints of too many other people. Nothing in the way of evidence there.

Moving to the door, Brackett checked the jamb, the hinges, and the door itself. Nothing there that could help. Before stepping through, he studied the carpeting from the door to where the body lay. She was on her back, her hands at her side. Her eyes were closed, but it was easy to see that she had been manually strangled.

"She's been moved," said Brackett.

"Yes," agreed Obo.

Brackett moved to the side and pointed. "You see anything on the carpet, on the body, that'll be damaged if we move on in?"

Obo crouched in the door and scanned the area. His eyesight, evolved on a world that had a slightly different atmospheric composition, with a star that gave off light in a slightly different range, could sometimes see things that the human eye could not.

He was quiet as he concentrated on the crime scene. Finally he said, "I see nothing."

"Okay," said Brackett. He moved in and knelt next to the body. He touched her hand and wrist and felt for the pulse that he knew would not be there. It was obvious that she was dead. The blackened and bloodied tongue pushing between her teeth told him that.

"Strangled," said Brackett.

"Yes."

He looked at the carpeting, at the scuff marks and footprints. He examined them on his hands and knees, getting his nose down so that it was only inches from the surface of the carpet. "Here. Looks like she fell, what? Right there. Profitt must have turned her over."

"Yes."

"Okay," said Brackett. "I want a crime team from the 107th down here immediately. Before the locals get in here and screw it up. I'll want the post done at the 107th where we've got the equipment."

There was a shout from down the hall. Loud voices, arguing. Brackett looked up at Obo and said, "Sounds like the police have arrived."

"You want that I should go stop them?"

"No," said Brackett, standing. "We'll just keep them out of here for a few minutes."

"Yes." Obo stepped into the hall, blocking it.

Brackett looked down at the body. A very good-looking woman who shouldn't be dead. He'd get to the bottom of it, if the local officials, Profitt, and Carnes would stay the hell out of the way.

He heard a voice he recognized as Hughes, screaming at Obo. "You get the hell out of the way, you big hairy beast. I'm here as a duly deputized officer of the law on this planet."

Obo said, "Please wait a moment."

Then another voice cut in. Tate said, "You've been avoiding me since we made planetfall. I have the permission of Captain Carnes to be here."

"You must wait for a moment."

"I've waited since I got here. I was promised cooperation if I cooperated. Now, I've spent my time in my room and getting my briefings from the locals," said Tate.

Brackett nodded to himself and thought that he hadn't played fair with Tate, but then the vidjournalists brought that on themselves. Too often they were wrapped up in their own self-importance, screaming that the people had a right to know when all they were doing was satisfying their own morbid curiosity about crime.

Obo repeated his order, his voice deepening as if he was getting angry. "You must wait a moment."

"Captain Carnes is going to hear all about this," said Tate. "Captain Carnes is not going to be pleased with the press coverage if I'm not allowed to get in there."

Brackett laughed and stood, thinking it was time to go stroke the ruffled feathers.

11 | Torch Song Trilogy

Lana stood in front of the full-length mirror that was fastened to the interior of the wardrobe, and watched as her body seemed to change shape. The mirror, cheap because the glass was flawed and cloudy, was good enough for her.

She turned slowly, looking at her back and butt and legs. Everything was perfect. It was always perfect. If something had been wrong, she would have been able to feel it. She didn't need visual confirmation of it, but then, there was never anything wrong.

Moving forward so that she could look into the wardrobe, she began to select the clothes for the evening's shows. Tonight she wanted something that showed her off because she was feeling exhibitionistic. She wanted the men, and some of the women, the few that came into the lounge, to see her in all her glory.

The dress she picked had very little material in it. Just enough to cover the parts that the bureaucrats had determined, through legislation, should be covered. She slipped into it, pulling it down over her head and then smoothing it so that it molded itself to her body.

Stepping back so that she could use the mirror, she saw that very little was left to the imagination. That was exactly the effect that she wanted to create. Now, add stockings, high heels, and the boys would be throwing themselves, and money, at her all night.

Dressed, she closed the wardrobe and moved to the door. She

surveyed the room quickly and shook her head. It was a good hiding place. It was the last place anyone would look.

She walked down the hallway, then the stairs and out, onto the street. There were few people on it. Most were hurrying home after working all day. Others were out, hoping for a breeze to cool them. Others sat, watching as the world passed them by.

Lana stopped near the car that had been parked by Ambassador Gleason. She used a key to unlock it, climbed behind the wheel, and started it. There was a roar as the fans began to rotate, lifting it from the cracked pavement of the street. No one paid the slightest attention to her. No one cared that the car had been parked by someone else. No one wanted to alert the police because the last thing any of them wanted was for the police to intrude on the serenity of the evening.

She drove down the street, turned, and entered the flow of traffic. She headed into the center of the city where there were high rises, hotels, shops, and restaurants. There were people who lived there, who made their living there, and hundreds of people who were passing through for one reason or another.

Lana pulled off the street, into a parking garage, and then descended. She found a parking place near the elevator where the light was the brightest. She locked the car and then walked to the elevator for a ride up. Sleeping in the small waiting area was a man in filthy clothes who smelled of vomit and cheap alcohol. Opportunities could be found throughout the city, but this man had somehow been overlooked.

She entered the elevator when it came and thought no more of the man lying on the concrete. Instead, she thought of Dennis Profitt, the richest man on the planet and the richest human in the known universe. Opportunity hadn't passed him by. Profitt, when opportunity appeared, had seized it, taking it for everything that he could.

She reached the surface and the door opened onto a covered mall area. All sorts of specialty shops lined the center court. A fountain sprayed water into the air and colored lights sparkled in it. A thousand people, most of them from other worlds, wandered the mall, looking for the souvenir that would best capture the trip here. Something unique that would cause friends to talk back home. Something that they, and ten million others, had.

Lana ignored them, walking slowly, letting the men watch her. She stepped on a slow-moving escalator and rode to the fourth floor where the Club BelaDona was just beginning to open its doors.

As she walked along, looking in windows that offered pastries, cookies, dresses, shoes, videos, or toys, she noticed the vidheadlines as they played across the screen. "DENNIS PROFITT INVOLVED IN THIRD DEATH IN TWO DAYS."

She stopped and stared at the screen, but the next headline told that production of the Southfork Mine had fallen for the third straight quarter, and that winds of more than two hundred miles an hour had destroyed a village on an island in the huge Mare Atlanta.

Grinning at the headlines, not of the poor production or the poor village, but of poor Dennis Profitt, she walked to the club. As the bouncer opened the door, Lana decided that she couldn't be happier. At last Profitt was getting some bad publicity.

Brackett stood outside the autopsy room, looking through the glass at the stainless-steel tables, floor, and fixtures. Linda Thoresson was stretched out on one, her clothing removed. Had it not been for the damage to her throat, and her tongue that no longer fit in her mouth, it would have been easy to believe that she was asleep.

Next to Brackett was Hughes, brought up at the insistence of the police commissioner planetside and Carnes who thought that it would improve their image with those below. Daily was preparing her report on her interview with Profitt, Obo was in the research facility, trying to learn something about the people from Fomalhaut Three. Both OBrien and Ryan were standing there waiting for the autopsy to begin.

Tate, his anger only slightly soothed, stood off to the side, watching what was happening inside the lab. Brackett hadn't wanted him there, but Hughes had asked Carnes if the reporter could attend. Carnes had said that he had no objections, so Tate was there, notebook in hand. Brackett had insisted that Tate not tape the autopsy. Even in death, people deserved a little dignity.

Hughes pulled a pack of cigarettes from his pocket and put one in his mouth.

"Smoking is restricted in the precinct," said Brackett.

"You can watch this without a cigarette to take your mind off what you're seeing?"

"Yeah," said Brackett.

"I'm impressed. Do you mind?"

Brackett was going to refuse to let him smoke but then Carnes's words came back to him. The captain had not been pleased with the altercation that had erupted in Profitt's penthouse when Brackett had refused to let Hughes and his officers inspect the body.

Hughes had demanded to be allowed in, but Obo, obeying the orders of his lieutenant, stood like a rock wall. Hughes finally gave up, and headed toward the living room to contact his superiors. While he was doing that, Brackett was trying to arrange for a crime team. He hoped that Daily was continuing her interview with Profitt. They'd need that information soon.

Brackett had succeeded in getting the team organized and cleared to use the port on the roof, but before they could arrive, Hughes managed to get an audience with Carnes. The situation changed radically and for the worse.

The solution was to allow Hughes and his people to attend the post done by the 107th. Their facilities, the most modern in that section of the galaxy, would be able to detect things that the locals might miss. Everyone would share the information and everyone would cooperate. Carnes and Commissioner Paul Landress of the local police had worked it out to their satisfaction.

So now Hughes, OBrien, and Ryan stood at the window and waited for the pathologist to enter and begin his work. They were also waiting for the technicians to arrive to prepare Linda Thoresson for the last thing she would ever do in front of an audience.

Tate had moved forward so that he could see better. He stood closer to Hughes and his people than to Brackett. Tate, in his way, was trying to express his displeasure with Brackett's attitude toward the working vidjournalists.

Hughes stood with the cigarette in his mouth, but hadn't lighted it. He was waiting to see what Brackett would say. Brackett, after all, was a lieutenant.

"If you need it," said Brackett. "By all means."

Hughes turned to OBrien and offered her one. She shook her head, refusing, and then suddenly thought better of it. She took a cigarette but didn't light it. Ryan declined the offer.

Two technicians appeared. Both were dressed in tight-fitting rubber suits. They wore masks over their faces. Brackett was never sure if they dressed that way to preserve the integrity of the evidence or if they were afraid of catching some deadly disease from the deceased.

"Here we go," he said.

One of the technicians used a holo camera to photograph the body, running it slowly from the top of her head all the way to her toes. As he finished, the second tech moved in and carefully examined her hands and fingers, then her throat, mouth, and ears. Using a probe, he prodded at her tongue and poked at the damage done to her throat. Apparently he found something embedded in the ruined tissues and used tweezers to remove it, placing it in a sterile glass container.

He repeated the procedure with the fingers, carefully scraping the area under the nails, placing the debris in glass containers, and then labeling each of them with a grease pencil.

When he completed the hands, he moved to the crotch, inspecting it carefully, but collecting no samples because there was no evidence that she had been sexually assaulted.

As he moved away, the first tech returned, turned the body over, and holoed it as slowly as he had the front. The second tech examined her back, her hair, and the bottoms of her feet, but again collected no samples.

"Not too bad," said OBrien. "Not what I expected."

Brackett shot a glance at her and then at Hughes. "She that new?"

"Afraid so."

"Wait," said Brackett.

Now the pathologist entered. He glanced at the window, recognized Brackett, and bowed, almost as if he were an actor taking the stage for the first time. He returned to the body that had been turned over so that it was on the back again. The pathologist examined her carefully, prodding at her, and then moved to the tray of tools that was sitting close to the table. He selected one carefully, held it up, as if to inspect it in the light, and then turned, plunging it into the chest of the body, as if he were planning on mutilating it.

"Oh," said OBrien, her face suddenly white.

The pathologist worked rapidly, opening the body from near the crotch to the breastbone. One of the technicians used snips to split the bone with a snap loud enough to be heard in the hallway.

Now Ryan was beginning to look green. He turned away, bent at the waist as if he were about to be sick, and then stood up, a hand clamped over his mouth. He ran down the hall, looking for a rest room.

The pathologist had seen that. He had been keeping an eye on the people outside. Through the speaker that was suddenly switched on, he said, "One down."

"Does he have to be so cavalier?" asked Hughes.

"You've been to an autopsy before, haven't you?" asked Brackett.

"Yeah," said Hughes, understanding. "Sometimes it seems that the pathologists are just trying to see how fast they can make everyone sick."

There was a strangled sound. Tate, his hand clamped to his mouth in an imitation of the pose last seen on Ryan, whirled and ran down the corridor.

Brackett turned to OBrien. "You're not required to be here. You might as well take off."

She glanced at him, as if to say that she could take anything that he could take. And then, beyond him, in the autopsy room, she saw the pathologist peel back the skin, opening up Thoresson's chest.

"Thanks," she said abruptly and then whirled, running after Ryan.

"Just the two of us," said Hughes.

Brackett nodded and touched a button that opened the intercom. "Just us professionals left, Doc. Do your damnedest now."

Brackett, along with Hughes and OBrien, was sitting in the Cup and Hole, looking out into space. They were on the side of the precinct away from the planet's surface. Brackett and Hughes were both drinking their coffee. OBrien's sat on the table in front of her untouched. She hadn't said more than a dozen words since they had entered the place.

"You seem to live pretty good up here," said Hughes, waving a hand to indicate the entire ship.

"Not the same as having a planet under your feet. Everyone is jammed in together, breathing recycled air and drinking recycled water."

"Still, it seems nicer than how eighty percent of the people on the planet live."

"You angling for an appointment to the precinct?" asked Brackett.

"Just commenting, is all."

"Applications are accepted at all times," pressed Brackett. "There's always the need for qualified, experienced officers."

"Maybe," said Hughes.

Before he could respond, one of the technicians appeared at the entrance of the Cup and Hole. He surveyed the crowd and then nodded at Brackett as he started over. Without sitting down, he said, "We've got some interesting preliminary results from the scrapings taken under the fingernails."

"Well?" said Brackett.

"Not human tissue." He grinned.

"I suppose that you can identify it," said Brackett. "Otherwise you wouldn't be standing there like an idiot."

"Of course I can identify it but I don't know if I want to if that's going to be your attitude."

"Shit," snapped Hughes.

"Patience, Sergeant," said Brackett. "You must allow the lab boys to have their moments of triumph. I believe he is going to now announce the name of the killer."

"I can narrow it down," said the technician. "It'll be up to you to take it the rest of the way."

"Come on, Beckley, give," said Brackett. "And if the information is as good as you're making out, I will personally buy you a cup of coffee and the largest pastry available in this very emporium."

Beckley pulled out a chair and dropped into it. "The tissue matches that of the residents of a faraway world that circles the star . . ." He hesitated, still grinning, and looking into the eyes of the other three. "Fomalhaut."

"Profitt's secretary," said Hughes immediately.

"You realize," said Beckley, "at the moment, I can't pinpoint a specific individual, but if you have a name, then we can make a DNA match once we gather the proper samples, and presto, we have a winner."

OBrien snapped, "This isn't the lottery."

Beckley looked hurt for just a moment and then said, "Almost."

Hughes rocked back in his chair and said, "She had the opportunity and it squares with what Profitt told your Sergeant Daily."

"Motive?" asked Brackett, though he had more than one idea about the motive.

Hughes shrugged. "Until we talk to her we can only guess. But I will say that if she's good for Thoresson, then she's probably good for the wife too."

"Which only leaves the robot and why it threw the man down the elevator shaft," said Brackett.

"I don't think that's related to these other events," said Hughes.

"No," said Brackett, "but once we clear that up, then we can get out of here."

Hughes nodded, hesitated, and then asked, "Who gets credit for solving this crime?"

"Well, it was our lab work that pointed the finger," said Brackett. "And our interview with Profitt that put the secretary in the right place."

"We could have done that," said Hughes.

Brackett agreed. "How about if we share the credit, with your names appearing first on the final report . . ."

"Works for me," said Hughes.

"The final report," repeated Brackett, "when we get around to writing it."

12 | The Origin of Species

Brackett and Hughes, back on the planet's surface, waited at the outside of the small, bricklike building in the dark. Neither stood close to the door, or any of the windows. OBrien and Ryan were covering the back, and Daily and Obo were stationed in a back alley, just in case.

"Do we know that she's in there?" asked Brackett.

"Everything suggests that she is."

"I would have thought that she'd live in the hotel where the corporate offices are."

Hughes shrugged. "I don't pretend to understand everything. I just know that she lives here and has ever since she arrived here. Lots of off-worlders live here."

Brackett said, "Everyone is set. Let's do it."

Hughes looked over his shoulder, at the hovercraft standing at the end of the street. A dozen officers from the local police force, outfitted for storming the building if there was a barricaded suspect, waited inside. They were the backup and the standby, in case the suspect turned out to be stronger or more desperate than anyone suspected.

Hughes moved forward and stepped up on the wraparound porch. He stayed away from the door, moved to the wall, and reached out, touching the knob. It twisted in his hand and the door opened easily.

Brackett touched the weapon tucked into a holster on his hip. Crouching slightly, he rushed through the door and into a hallway that was narrow but brightly lighted. The floor was carpeted and though a little worn, it was clean. Rows of doors lined the hallway.

"Number twelve," said Hughes, joining Brackett on the inside.

Brackett glanced at the door closest to him. That was number five. He pointed. "Down there?"

Hughes passed him. He drew his weapon and held it with the barrel pointed up, at the ceiling. He found the right door and stopped next to it. He pointed and lowered his voice, whispering, "This is it."

Brackett nodded and used his hand-held radio. "All units. All units. We're about to go in. Stand by." He moved around so that he was on the other side of the door and then waited for Hughes.

Hughes reached out from his position on the left side of the door and knocked. The button camera over the door came on, but showed neither of the police officers. From the tiny speaker came, "Who's there?"

"Police. Open up."

"I need to see a badge."

Hughes reached into his rear pocket, pulled his out, and flipped it open so that both the badge and the holo of him were visible.

"I need to see a person."

Hughes hesitated and then centered himself in front of the door. He held his hand to his side, his weapon slightly concealed and pointed at the floor.

"Okay."

Hughes glanced at Brackett but didn't move. He heard the lock click and the door open. The suspect stood in front of him, dressed in a short robe, a towel wrapped around her head.

"Are you Rachel de vo Willom?"

"Yes."

"Private secretary to Dennis Profitt?"

"What is this all about?"

Hughes touched a pocket in his suit jacket and said, "I have a warrant for your arrest on the suspicion of murder of an intelligent being, in this case a human being. I should warn you that you have the right to remain silent and you have a right to an attorney if you want legal representation."

Brackett hadn't moved as he listened to Hughes recite the laws under the current planetary government. He was watching the woman's face, looking for some sign of emotion. With humans, he could often read in their faces what they felt, but some of the alien races were next to impossible to read. They managed to keep everything hidden, or the expression of emotion was different than what would be expected from humans.

"I would like to call Mr. Profitt," she said.

"When we get to the station."

"I'd like to call him now," she insisted.

"I'm afraid that won't be possible."

"When Mr. Profitt learns what has happened, he's going to be angry."

Now Brackett spoke. "I'm afraid that we're not interested in Mr. Profitt's reactions to this. If we're wrong, we will apologize and do what is necessary to make the situation right. However, at the moment, you are under arrest. I would suggest that you find some suitable clothing and prepare to come with us."

She seemed to understand that she was wearing only the short robe. She grabbed the material at the throat and held it closed. "A moment." She turned.

Hughes followed her. "I'm afraid that we'll have to accompany you."

Brackett waited until the both of them had cleared the doorway and then entered the apartment. He was surprised by the interior. On the floor, near what looked to be a rubber couch, was a small, shallow pool. Lily pads floated in it.

The interior was hot and humid. Brackett was aware of sweat forming and beginning to drip. He said nothing, staying out of the way and allowing Hughes to make the arrest.

Rachel moved toward a wide door, let it open for her, and then stopped. "This is my sleeping chamber."

"I'm afraid that I can't allow you in there without escort," said Hughes.

"On my world, such a request by a stranger would be met with death."

"We're not on your world," said Hughes, "and it's interesting that you express such violence."

"You will follow?"

"I can stand at the door," said Hughes, "but I must keep you in sight."

She looked beyond him, to Brackett, as if appealing to a higher authority. Brackett said nothing. She waited and when she decided that she was going to get no help from him, she shrugged. She opened her robe and let it fall to her feet.

Brackett was surprised that she looked so human. Had it not been for the lack of hair and the leathery texture of the skin, he would have thought that she was Oriental.

She seemed unconcerned with her nudity now. She turned slowly and walked into the other room. Hughes followed her, stopping at the door as he said he would.

Under other circumstances, Brackett would have been concerned about it. A suspect who was allowed to walk into a back room was inviting trouble. There could be weapons stashed, other people hidden to assist in an escape, or a dozen other complications. But Brackett, watching her, didn't think that was going to happen. There was no real reason to be suspicious of her actions. Because of that, he let Hughes run the operation without checking the room.

"Take what you'll need to be gone for about a day," said Hughes.

Brackett stood and moved to the shallow pool in front of the couch. He crouched in front of it and then dipped a hand into the water. It was warm, almost hot. There was a swirl on the surface, and he spotted a fish snap its tail as it dived deeper.

Humans raised on Earth liked to have warm, dry environments, though they created other environments that allowed them to re-create some of the conditions found outside. Why shouldn't beings raised on a marsh world prefer to live in humid, wet surroundings.

Hughes stepped back, into the main room, but kept his eyes

on the woman. She entered, now dressed in a more conventional fashion. The narrow skirt brushed her knees, and the blouse buttoned to the throat.

"I'm ready," she said.

Hughes looked at her and said, "Please turn around. Hands behind your back."

"Is that necessary?"

"Standard procedure," said Hughes.

She looked at Brackett as if to again appeal the situation. Brackett shrugged. When procedure was violated, for whatever reason, police officers got killed. Cut a suspect a break and it could be the last time.

Finally she did as requested. Hughes used his cuffs, snugging them down so that her thin hands couldn't slip through, freeing her.

Using the radio, Brackett said, "We have the suspect in custody and we're coming out."

"Understood."

Before any of them moved, the woman said, "If you'd allow me to call Mr. Profit, all this trouble could be avoided."

"It's no trouble," said Hughes.

"Not yet," she said.

Lab work took a long time, even with the computers and other equipment that were used on the 107th. There were so many variables, so many things to look for, so much evidence that had to be found, cataloged, examined, and added to the data base that small things could sometimes be overlooked in the preliminary rush. That was why, after the preliminaries were completed, the longer, slower work began.

Beckley, working alone in his lab, was comparing the cell samples taken from the scrapings under Linda Thoresson's fingernails with the genetic makeup of the beings that lived on Fomalhaut Three.

And as he studied the samples, he found that there were irregularities that just didn't fit. The genetic material, examined in the extreme by one of the most powerful electron microscopes available, yielded results that made him regret his attitude when he'd made the announcement to Brackett and the officers from the planet's surface.

The cellular material was a close match to that of the representative sample from Fomalhaut Three. But close didn't make it. Or rather, this was not close enough to fall within the normal differences of the genetic makeup of someone who had been born on Fomalhaut Three. Even interbreeding, which would change the genetic characteristics to a small extent, couldn't explain the discrepancy.

Beckley spun away from the eyepieces and rolled his chair across the tile floor, using his feet to pull himself along. He stopped in front of a computer, sat for a moment, thinking, and then reached for the keyboard, pulling it close, typing in his question.

The screen went blank except for the cursor that flashed. Suddenly it said, "Working." Finally it said, "No matches available."

Beckley sat back and contemplated the implications of that. It meant that the genetic material was unique. Then, grinning, he realized that it couldn't be unique. There had to be a match somewhere. There might not be one in his computer bank, but there would be one available somewhere.

The pathologist, George Denvers, entered, saw Beckley sitting in front of the computer, and asked, "What's the matter now?"

"No genetic match."

"Thought you had one."

"So did I, but it falls outside the acceptable parameters. Had to reevaluate it. I'm no longer sure that Fomalhaut Three is the right answer."

Denvers shook his head and said, "Brackett's not going to be happy."

"Well, he shouldn't expect us to hand him the answer on a silver platter."

Denvers took off his bloodstained lab coat and hung it on the hook near the door. "I'm going to get something to eat. You about done here?"

"Shouldn't we let Brackett know that we've run into trouble here?" asked Beckley.

"Let's get the completed report and then let's tell him. Brackett knows that the preliminary findings are just that. Preliminary."

"Okay, but he's not going to be happy."

Denvers walked over and looked into the electron microscope. He sat down in front of it, twisted around. He studied the sample for a moment and asked, "Are you sure that these are the cells that you scraped from the post?"

"Sure." He pointed to the glass container. "Got them right out of there."

"Well, I don't know why you thought they matched those from Fomalhaut Three. These aren't even close." Denvers looked up at Beckley.

"What?" Beckley moved to the scope and took another look. He could easily see that the cellular material looked as if it had come from a human from Earth.

"I don't understand this," he said, shaking his head. He glanced at Denvers and then added, "No. I wouldn't make a mistake like that."

"Then the only conclusion that can be drawn is that your sample changed itself. Restructured itself, even under the intense bombardment that should have killed it if it was still alive."

"No," said Beckley. For a moment he wondered if it could have mutated, but realized that couldn't be. The cells themselves wouldn't change. The mutations would become evident as the cells divided, but the old cells would still be in evidence. It looked as if the cells themselves had changed and Beckley knew that was impossible.

13 | Good Cop and Bad Cop

Rachel de vo Willom sat in the tiny, brightly lighted, and cold cubicle, waiting. She had been waiting for nearly an hour. She'd been left alone, her hands still cuffed behind her, in the cold room, while the police officers did something else.

She was smart enough to know what was happening. The police were trying to soften her up. They were allowing her to stew in her own juices, thinking about why she had been arrested, why they had brought her here, and about what would happen to her in the future. Had she been guilty, it might have worked.

When the door opened she felt like grinning but knew that the cops would not understand that reaction. Instead, she sat with her head down, staring at the abused table that was in front of her.

Hughes was the first in. He pulled out the chair opposite her and sat down. Brackett stood in the rear, leaning against the wall, his arms folded. He didn't say anything.

"You have not allowed me to call Mr. Profitt," she said.

"In a moment. There are some questions that we want to ask you first."

"Why don't you remove the cuffs?" said Brackett.

Hughes shot him an angry glance, but stood and walked around the table. He used a key and unlocked them.

"Thanks," she said. "Now my call?"

Hughes dropped into his chair and leaned his elbows forward, on the small table that separated them. "Let's just cut the crap. We've got a witness to you running from Profitt's apartment and we've got physical evidence linking you to the murder of Linda Thoresson."

There was a moment of silence. She sat perfectly still, almost like a small creature that had seen the shadow of a predator flash by. She stared at him, her eyes unblinking. There was nothing in her reaction or her facial expressions to suggest that she was worried about what Hughes had said.

"You have a comment?" asked Hughes.

"I want to call Mr. Profitt."

"He's the one who ID'ed you as you ran from the penthouse after killing Thoresson."

"I have no reason to kill anyone."

There was a tap on the door and Brackett turned to open it. Daily poked her head in. "Can I see you a moment, Loot?"

To Hughes, Brackett said, "I'll be right back."

Hughes ignored him, keeping his attention on Willom.

Outside the cubicle, Brackett said, "What you got?"

Daily rubbed her chin and said, "Word from the 107th. Seems your friend Beckley was a little quick to make his pronouncement."

"Meaning?"

"Cell samples do not match those of the residents of Fomalhaut Three."

"Meaning," said Brackett, "that the physical evidence linking our suspect with the crime has just evaporated."

"Couple that to what Profitt told me, that is, that he wasn't sure that it was her, and that the computer records checked showed that she was at her desk just as she was supposed to be, and we've got nothing."

"A good attorney would get us thrown out in a minute," said Brackett.

"Hell, Loot, a good attorney would keep this thing from ever going to trial."

"Well," said Brackett, "I thought that we were wrapping this up too easily."

"Our next move?"

"We'll work that out later. I'd better keep Hughes from making it any worse than it is. Thanks." He turned and entered the cubicle.

Hughes was standing, his hands flat on the table, looking down at Willom. His voice was louder, but he wasn't shouting, just emphasizing his words. "Why don't you help us out and things will go easier on you."

"Sergeant," said Brackett, "I think that we've taken too much of Ms. Willom's time. She's been most cooperative. Maybe we should just escort her home."

Hughes whirled, his face a sudden mask of rage that disappeared quickly. He hesitated and then, picking up the ball, said, "Maybe you'd like to make your phone call now?"

"If I'm going to be taken home, I think that I'd rather do that. The call won't be necessary."

Brackett moved closer and held out a hand as if wanting to assist her. "We certainly appreciate your time here. And your cooperation."

She wasn't fooled by the sudden kindness. She looked from Hughes, who had been building in his role as the bad cop, but who had been cut down, and then at Brackett. "What happened?"

Brackett grinned broadly and said, "In police work, we must often follow trails that lead us in the wrong direction. Because we often deal with individuals whose concept of right and wrong doesn't agree with ours, it means that we must follow our standard procedures. Such procedures protect both the police officer and the suspect."

"That doesn't tell me what happened."

"No. We had some very good reasons to suspect you. Unfortunately . . . or maybe I should say fortunately for you, those reasons have now evaporated. Rather than keep you here unnecessarily and inconveniencing you further, we decided that we'd just take you back to your apartment."

For a moment she stood still. Finally she nodded and said, "That would be nice."

"I'll have one of the other officers escort you," said Brackett.

"No. I believe that I'd like you to do it."

"Certainly."

She headed toward the door. "You've been very kind, considering, though I didn't appreciate your comments about Mr. Profitt."

Brackett laughed. "You'd be surprised how often our"—he shrugged helplessly—"suspect attempts to invoke the name of a powerful friend, acquaintance, or relative. We must ignore that to do our job."

"Certainly," she said. "Now, if we might hurry."

Brackett glanced at Hughes and said, "Of course."

Lana stood on the stage, looking into the blaze of the spotlights, trying to see beyond the glare and into the faces of the men and women who were watching. She whirled once and then danced to the edge of the narrow platform that served as a stage for the club. The music, artificial, blared from speakers behind her, giving the impression that the band was hidden behind the curtains though there was no band.

Using the microphone as a prop, Lana dropped to her knees and leaned back until the top of her head touched the floor. All the time she continued to sing.

She slipped to the right, stretching out on the stage, and then rolled to her back. She lifted her legs, her knees straight. Finally she let her feet touch the floor, spun again, and stood, leaning forward, into the light so that the tops of her breasts were highlighted.

The crowd might not have known good music, but they understood the erotic nature of the dance. Several of them were standing, screaming their approval.

The song ended and Lana decided that she'd had enough. Three hours on the stage, dancing and singing, sapped her strength. Her bones ached. It was time to give it up for the night, no matter how loud the audience cheered or how much money they tossed.

She stood up straight, faced them, bowed at the waist, turned to the right, bowed, and then turned to the left. She set the microphone on the floor, leapt to the rear, and disappeared through the curtains.

"That was great," said Osbourne, the club's manager. "You got them screaming out there, wanting more, and sucking down the booze like there's no tomorrow."

"I'm beat," she said.

"Can't talk you into another quick set? Thirty minutes. Give you a big bonus." Osbourne suddenly realized that he was still holding the towel he'd brought for her and held it out.

Gratefully, Lana took it and mopped her face, chest, and then under her arms. "I'm really beat."

"You did put it all into the show. One hell of a performance tonight."

"Was he here?" she asked.

Osbourne shrugged. "I don't know. I didn't look."

"Come on, Jerry. You know. No one lets a man like Profitt sneak in without knowing it. If he was here, you know."

"Yeah. He was here. Watched for a few minutes and then slipped out the rear."

"Damn," she said.

"There's a lot going on around him," said Osbourne. "All the time."

Lana nodded and said, "I'm about to collapse."

"Then go on home. I'll bring on the second-string. She doesn't sing or dance as well, but she'll take off every stitch that she's wearing. Kind of makes up for a second-rate voice."

Lana stepped to the rear and slumped into the rickety chair sitting there. She wiped her face again. Her hair was sweat-damp, feeling as if she'd just stepped out of the shower.

"You go on home," said Osbourne. "You earned your money tonight."

"You're sure that he left?"

"I'm sure that he's no longer in the club. Doesn't mean that he's not waiting outside for you," said Osbourne.

Lana leaned forward, her elbows on her knees, and held the

towel up to dry her face. "I just wish he'd come backstage to say something."

"Why?"

"Don't be an ass. The man has more money than God."

"Oh." He stood silently for a moment and then said, "I'd better warn Sarah that she's on in a few minutes. Give her a chance to get ready."

"She's always ready."

"True."

Osbourne pushed his way through the beaded curtain and disappeared down the narrow hall. Lana sat for a moment, cooling down and listening as the music started again. The speakers shook the back room. The walls vibrated in time to the beat. It was beginning to make her sick.

She stood up and left the little room. She stopped at the door, opened it, and looked out, into the club. The tables were jampacked. Men had filtered into the front so that they could see better. By leaning to the right, she could see the stage. Sarah was up there, beginning her routine. Already she'd managed to lose her skirt and blouse.

Lana let the door shut and continued down the hallway, using the side exit to leave the club. She wanted to avoid the men and women inside. Now she was only interested in getting away from there. Outside, in the mall, she turned and looked at the line of people waiting to enter. She scanned them but saw no one she recognized. Profitt, if he had stayed, had found somewhere else to hide.

She took the escalator down, surveying the floors as she did. At the ground level, she walked to the elevator and took it down to her car. The drunk who had been sprawled on the floor just outside the elevator hadn't moved. He cradled a bottle like it was a baby.

She stepped around him and hurried to her hover car. No one was following her. The underground parking area was brightly lighted to inhibit crime.

She unlocked the car and climbed in, starting it. After checking the area around her carefully, she backed out, slipped into forward, and drove up the ramp, exiting onto the main street. Now that it was after midnight, the traffic had thinned. Too many people had jobs that required them to arrive early. Most people were home.

On the street, she checked the mirrors to make sure that she wasn't being followed. Without much traffic, it was an easy thing to do. Satisfied, she drove to the Star Rest Hotel, cruised the front, but didn't stop. She pulled away from it, into the park opposite, and found a place to stop. Sitting in her car, she could look up at the high rise climbing up into the star-spangled night.

On the top of the building was the penthouse where Profitt lived. The lights were on but she knew that meant nothing. Profitt had enough money to let the lights burn if he wanted. Or it meant that the staff was there waiting for his return. Lights on in the penthouse meant nothing.

She sat there for a moment, watching. There were things that had to be done. Things that could wait no longer. Now she had to get busy.

14 | When All Else Fails, Start Over and Follow the Directions

"With our only suspect eliminated," said Hughes, standing in front of the others, "there is only one thing to do."

Brackett, who'd delivered Rachel de vo Willom to her apartment and rushed back, said, "I think that we must examine the facts again. All the facts, beginning with the death at the hands of the robot."

"That's not related," said Hughes.

"We have a man killed in the same hotel only a few hours before Janet Profitt is found dead."

"You suggesting he killed Janet Profitt?"

Brackett shook his head. "I think everything indicates that he was intercepted on his way up rather than on his way down. I just find it strange that he was killed just hours earlier."

"So what do we do?" asked OBrien.

"Prepare a list of suspects," said Brackett. "As I understand it, Profitt and Klaus found Janet Profitt. They are on the list."

Hughes was quiet for a moment and then said, "I'd like to add Ambassador Sumner Gleason to that list. I found him standing over the body."

"But after you'd already seen it," said Brackett.

"Still, he appeared on the scene quickly."

"I never said he shouldn't be added," said Brackett, "I was only trying to fit that into the time frame."

Now Daily spoke. "And Profitt again. He found Thoresson. That's two, in his penthouse. He should be at the top of the list."

"I don't like that," said Brackett, "because it's so obvious. If he was the killer, would he be that obvious? Suspicion falls on him automatically."

"Maybe that's the kind of thinking he's counting on," said Daily.

Brackett looked at Hughes, aware of the blurred lines of command. Hughes was the senior local police official but Brackett, with his interplanetary jurisdiction, could take command without worrying about being overruled until someone with higher rank stepped in.

When Hughes didn't speak, Brackett said, "I think that we need to investigate the background of Klaus, and the two male instructors who worked closely with Janet Profitt." Glancing at Hughes, he added, "The ambassador, the private secretary, and O'Shaughnessy. I want to know what he was doing there."

"What about Janet Profitt and Linda Thoresson?" asked Daily.

"Good point," said Brackett. "There anything in their backgrounds? There a point where they came together before Profitt married the one and hired the other?"

"There's not necessarily a connection," said Hughes.

"No," said Brackett, "but there might be and we can't let any stone go unturned."

"What about his private secretary?" asked OBrien.

"Let's learn what we can about her," said Brackett. "Our evidence against her fell apart, but that doesn't automatically eliminate her from the running. She just tumbles down the list of suspects."

It was too late that night to begin anything useful, except make sure that Profitt was in his penthouse and that he didn't go anywhere that evening. Hughes and his people said that it was their planet and they would take care of it.

With that decided, Brackett suggested that they all get some sleep and start again, early in the morning. They'd be there about seven to coordinate the surveillance that would begin on the main suspects.

Brackett, Daily, and Obo left the station house, walking. They all had wanted to walk, to burn off some of the excess energy. Besides, it wasn't that far to the hotel.

Obo, who was fascinated by everything that he could see, as if he'd never been on a civilized planet, trailed along behind them.

Daily tried to slow the pace. She looked into a window that held several necklaces. A tiny spotlight shined down on a brilliant green stone that seemed to glow with its own internal illumination. She stopped to look.

"Gemstone," said Brackett.

"Beautiful," she said.

Brackett turned away and began to stroll down the street. He noticed that there weren't many people. The stores, shops, and the restaurants were all closed. There was a corner store that was brightly lighted but there didn't seem to be anyone inside it.

"I'm not very tired," said Daily. "Even with everything that has happened tonight, I'm not tired."

Brackett laughed. "I'm about to drop. There's something about changing from the artificial atmosphere of the precinct to the natural environment of a planet that tires me out. They used to call it jet lag. Crossing too many time zones on a planet would wear out a person. A psychological problem, I guess."

She moved closer to him so that her hip bumped against his. "I've never had that problem. It always seems to, what, excite me as we land on a new planet."

They came to a street and stopped, watching the sporadic traffic. A hover car drifted along slowly. It stopped once, and then accelerated. There was nothing else moving along the street.

"Let's go, Obo," said Brackett.

"He'll be okay," said Daily. "He's big enough to take care of himself."

"You might not have noticed, but there is a real distrust of aliens."

"Nothing physical," said Daily. "Besides, he's a police officer. Which reminds me. What happened to Tate?"

"He decided to remain back on the ship." Brackett laughed. "I think he was mad because we tended to ignore him once we got to the planet's surface."

"You think he'll cause us any trouble? He knows quite a bit now."

"No," said Brackett. "He knows this is a two-way street. If he screws over us, word will get out and that'll be the end of cooperation by any of the officers. He'd do it for one giant story, but this doesn't qualify."

"We've got Profitt," said Daily.

"I mean, it's not the kind of thing that would be worth burning all his sources to get. This case is a good week in the vids and that's all. It's not the kind to make a career."

"Yeah. Well, I'm not unhappy to have him remain behind," said Daily. Without thinking, she took his hand and almost dragged him across the street. She stopped in front of the lighted store, peering in the window.

It was a small store that catered to those who were staying in the hotels and who might have a midnight craving for a snack, a bottle of booze, a newspaper, or a magazine.

"Want to go in and look around?"

"At what?" asked Brackett. "Candy bars and newspapers? I think we'd better just get back to the hotel and get some rest. We're going to be busy tomorrow."

Obo caught them, looked through the window for a moment, and then started off down the street, as if to lead them. He didn't say a word.

Brackett started to follow, and then turned to look at Daily. "You coming?"

"There's no hurry," said Daily. "We should get some time off, you know."

"Not once we've made planetfall. Then we have an obligation to complete the job as quickly as possible. Besides, we've got three dead bodies."

"But it's not as if we're chasing a serial killer. Where will he strike next? Is anyone safe? Apparently, if you're not on the upper floors or in the penthouse of the Star Rest, then you're safe."

"Which takes it all right to Profitt's front door. Maybe we should go ask him some pointed questions."

"I did that. You read the report?"

"Scanned it," said Brackett.

Daily stopped and turned, looking into a darkened window. The conversation wasn't going in the direction she wanted it to go. She was trying to recapture the moments in the Off-Duty but couldn't get Brackett to respond to the personal comments. He kept deflecting them with discussions of the case.

"He claims to have found the bodies, both times," said Brackett. "Including one in a locked room. A room that they had to break into."

"According to OBrien and Ryan, Klaus backs up that story and they both say that the physical evidence supports the view." She looked at Brackett and wondered how he'd dragged her into a discussion of the case so quickly and so easily. It wasn't something that she wanted to talk about.

"And Profitt was home alone when he discovered the body of Thoresson. He mention why there were no servants or staff there with him?"

"He gave the staff the day off. After what had happened the night before, he felt that they should be allowed to go home, and mourn in their own way."

"Live-in staff?"

"Very few," said Daily. "And they had families to visit. Profitt tried to maintain a . . . no, that's not quite fair. He went to work as normal. I don't think we can draw conclusions from that."

They crossed the street, turned, and in front of them was the hotel. Light spilled from the windows and the doors. A single man dressed in a long, brightly colored coat stood, waiting for the guests to arrive.

"We haven't done much," said Brackett. "Profitt, because of his proximity to the crimes, has to be the number one suspect. Klaus is right up there, but then, he wasn't close for the second or third death, depending on if we count the robot."

"So what do we do?"

"Ask questions. Stir around. See what floats to the surface. Maybe find someone who looks good, on a computer screen, for the crimes and pretend that we're convinced he or she's the one. Divert attention from Profitt."

"Motive?" asked Daily.

"That's the problem, isn't it? We get the motive and I think we'll have the answer."

They reached the hotel. The doorman opened the door and bowed as they entered. In the lobby, they found Obo sitting on a couch, waiting.

He stood. "I have waited."

Brackett yawned. "I think that we all had better get some sleep. Get started early in the morning."

"I've a bottle in my room," said Daily, looking pointedly at Brackett.

"I go to my room to sleep," said Obo.

"Loot?"

Brackett suddenly understood what was happening and wondered why he'd been so slow. Maybe it was because he was tired. More likely it was because he didn't want to see. A relationship, no matter how platonic, could cause all sorts of complications and he wasn't sure that he wanted to deal with them.

"I think that I need to catch some sleep," said Brackett.

"One drink."

Obo stood waiting for a moment and then turned, walking toward the elevators.

"One drink," repeated Daily.

"Sure," said Brackett, caving in.

They followed Obo across the lobby. The elevator arrived, Obo entered it, and then held the door for them. They entered and Obo pushed the button.

They rode up without talking. The doors opened and they all exited. As they started down the hall, Obo said, "I think I would like a drink."

Daily shot him a glance, but now there was no way to refuse. She'd invited him earlier. "Sure," she said.

Brackett laughed and then said, "I think I'll just go on to bed."

"Fine," said Daily. "You do that."

"Good night, Loot," said Obo.

Profitt, a drink in his hand, wandered around the living room, stopping at the French doors that led out onto the deck that overlooked the city, and then back into the penthouse. He touched the controls that would start the music, shut it off, activated the video wall, and watched as a man shot down a snowy mountain, dodging in and out of artificial gates, and then slid to a stop across a finish line. He cycled through the channels, looking for something but finding nothing interesting. Or rather, nothing that interested him.

He walked back to the French doors and stopped. There was a quiet chiming, telling him that someone was at the front door at the lower level. Raising his voice because he knew he was alone, he called, "Who's there?"

"Father Robert."

"Father? What are you doing here so late?" asked Profitt, surprised.

"I thought that a few words might provide you with some comfort."

Profitt set his drink on the closest table and then walked to the control panel. "I'll buzz you in, Father."

"Thank you."

As soon as Father Robert had entered, Profitt made sure that the front door was locked and then hurried to the head of the stairs to intercept the priest.

"I appreciate your coming," said Profitt as Father Robert climbed the steps, "but it wasn't necessary."

"Of course it was. Tragedy has touched your doorstep twice in the last few days."

"Would you care for a drink?"

"Wine."

Profitt moved to one of the wet bars, bent down, and looked at the bottles stacked under the sink. He took one out, set it on the bar, and then opened it carefully. "Need to let it breathe for a moment."

"Of course."

Profitt sat down on the couch and then said, "Have a seat, Father."

The priest stood for a moment with his back to the room, staring out into the night sky. His hands were clasped behind his back as he rocked on his heels and toes. Without turning, he said, "I have the feeling that you're not as happy as you once were."

"My wife is dead," said Profitt automatically. "And one of my employees."

Turning, Father Robert said, "But I have the feeling there is something more here. Something that is buried just beneath the surface of your consciousness. Something that ties all this together and that once it is out in the open, then life can return to what it was."

Profitt looked down at the thick carpet. "I had nothing to do with either of those deaths."

"I know, my son, but we reap what we sow."

"Meaning what?" asked Profitt.

"Can any of us say that we've done nothing that doesn't cry out for forgiveness?"

Profitt stared at the priest and then stood, walking to the bar. "Wine?"

"You're nervous, my son."

"No, Father, not nervous. Frightened. There is something going on here that I don't understand. Something is happening and I can't do a thing about it."

"What have you done in the past?" asked the priest, his voice quiet, as if in the confessional. "Is there anything that you've done in your life that you haven't admitted to yourself or God?"

For a moment an image flashed in his mind, but Profitt suppressed it quickly. Totally. It had been so long ago. It was something that he no longer thought about. It was something that had nothing to do with his life anymore. It was something that he'd rather not think about anymore.

"Confession," said Father Robert, "is very good for the soul."

Profitt concentrated on pouring the wine into the small crystal glass. He carried it to the priest. As he handed it over, he said, "I've done nothing to be ashamed of. Nothing that hasn't been told."

"Are you positive, my son?"

Staring up, out the French doors, Profitt lied, "Yes, Father, I'm sure."

15 | The Check Is in the Mail

The quiet beeping on the up-link to the 107th woke Brackett just before dawn. At first he didn't know where he was, what he had been doing, and the line of light from the bathroom off to his right scared him. For a moment he didn't know who would come out of there.

Then he remembered that he'd passed on Daily's offer of a late-night drink and headed down to his room alone. There was no one in the bathroom. He must have left the light on himself the night before.

The beeping came again and he rolled over, tried to find his watch, dropped it, and then looked at the curtains over the window. Though they were heavy, he could see the light bleeding around the edges.

He forced himself out of bed, padded to the table, and dropped into one of the chairs. He noticed that it was cold in the room. Air-conditioning was working well. He shivered as he reached up, touched the keyboard, and acknowledged that he was ready.

The screen filled and the internal printer began to spit out the hard copy. Brackett tried to read the screen but he couldn't focus on it. His eyes kept blurring on him.

He stood up and walked to the bathroom, confirmed that it was empty, and then bent over the sink to splash water on his face. He held a hand under the faucet, drank, and then straightened. As he grabbed a towel, the buzzer on the up-link sounded indicating that there was a verbal message.

Brackett walked back into the bedroom, touched the button at the side of the up-link that cleared the screen, and then sat down.

Denvers, the pathologist, appeared. He stared at Brackett and then said, "You look horrible."

"Thanks. What are you doing awake so early?"

"We never sleep. Unheralded, unsung, we provide the clues that allow you to solve the cases and crush crime and your only question is what am I doing awake so early."

"I hope, whatever it is, it's better than what Beckley gave me."

"We're still at a loss to explain how that could have gone so very wrong . . ."

Brackett closed his eyes and waved a hand at the screen. Opening his eyes, he asked, "What do you have?"

"Your man, O'Shaughnessy . . ."

"The robed religious nut that got himself tossed down the elevator shaft."

"The very same."

"What about him?" asked Brackett, not sure that he cared any longer.

"The robot has been cleared of any wrongdoing, if a robot can do wrong. We've been able, finally, to establish the man's real identity. His cover was virtually perfect. That's what gave us fits. However, one of his cornea transplants was jarred . . . would that be the right word? Jarred? Anyway, it was detached by the impact of the body at the bottom of the shaft. We spotted that and were able to detect enough of his original corneas so that we could get a match."

Brackett was suddenly wide awake, his eyes completely focused. "Who was it?"

"Small-time hood, professional killer, named Richard Holtz. Made his living for the last twelve, fifteen years by killing for hire."

"So I guess the robot can be released to its owner . . ."

"One Dennis Profitt," said Denvers.

"Can we assume," said Brackett, thinking out loud, "that Profitt was the target?"

"We could," said Denvers, "though there is no evidence that he was."

"Interesting that we've a hired assassin coming in, then, hours later, Janet Profitt dies and the next day Linda Thoresson is killed."

"Yes," said Denvers.

Brackett was quiet for a moment, rubbed a hand through his hair trying to smooth it, and asked, "We know why the robot attacked the man? He wasn't carrying a weapon, according to the police reports."

"There we get into an area of speculation," said Denvers, "but, as you know, the Bodyguard 4000 series has fine detection and discrimination capabilities. Without those capabilities, the Bodyguard 4000 wouldn't be worth much. I suspect that it detected the tampering done with the cornea, the extra padding that had been injected into the body to add to the look of obesity, and the fact that O'Shaughnessy had engaged in sexual intercourse in the few hours prior to his demise."

"Now how in the hell could you tell that?" asked Brackett.

"You want the clinical answer?"

"No."

"Let's just say that such activity leaves a residue that is detectable if suitable external protection is not used. Apparently our Mr. O'Shaughnessy believed in the old adage 'I'm not going to do it wearing a sock.' "

"And the robot would have picked up on that?"

"Certainly. Couple it all to the fact that the O'Shaughnessy splinter sect believes in abstinence, there were certainly enough clues for the robot to act."

Brackett took a deep breath and leaned back in the chair, pinching the bridge of his nose. "That was a fairly final act, wasn't it."

"I think the point," said Denvers, "is that the robot was correct in its assessment of the situation. It killed an assassin proving that it was right."

"And I suppose if you're Dennis Profitt you can get away with having a Bodyguard 4000."

"Thought you'd want the latest," said Denvers.

"Yeah. Thanks."

"If I might make a suggestion. Get to bed earlier. You need to get sufficient sleep."

"It's the planetfall," said Brackett. "Plays havoc on the body for the first couple of days."

"See the medical examiner when you come back to the ship. I think he's got something that'll reduce the effects."

"Sure," said Brackett. "Oh, you got anything on the background of this . . . what? Holtz."

"Fed through to you."

"I don't suppose we know who hired him?"

"Research is working on that, but on these frontier worlds not all the computer, interplanetary phone, and communications are monitored as closely as we'd like."

"I suppose that we could drop the name around and see who reacts to it," said Brackett. "Thanks."

"You're welcome." The screen faded.

Brackett stood up, stretched then, but before he could get into the bathroom, there was a knock at the door. "Yeah?"

"You said that we'd meet for breakfast."

Brackett walked to the door, unlocked it, and then opened it. Daily pushed her way through, looked at him standing there in his underwear, and said, "You look horrible."

"Thanks."

"And you're late."

"Nope," said Brackett. "Working." He hitchhiked a thumb at the up-link. "Got a report on the robot and O'Shaughnessy. Why don't you take a look at it while I grab a shower?"

"Need some help?" asked Daily, grinning evilly.

"You should be careful about making remarks like that. Someday someone is going to take you up on it."

She walked over to the table and looked at the pile of paper behind the up-link. Turning, she said, "Sure they are. I keep making the offer but no one seems interested."

Brackett yawned again and rubbed a hand over the stubble on his face. Sometimes he wondered why he didn't have the problem removed for all time. There were ways of permanently stopping the growth of his beard. Unfortunately none were reversible and sometimes it helped to have two or three days growth.

He scratched at his bare chest and said, "Read the damned report and I'll be ready in fifteen minutes."

"Sure, Loot. Whatever you say."

Profitt had not slept during the night. Father Robert's visit had bothered him, not because he was responsible for the deaths of either Janet or Linda Thoresson, but because the priest had suggested that it was retribution for some past transgression.

And it wasn't a past transgression that worried him. He'd made his peace twenty years ago. The situation had worked out so that he survived and became, at that time, the richest creature in the known universe. He didn't even care when the slug had passed him, leaving him as only the richest human. That was enough for Profitt.

No, what bothered him was that Father Robert seemed to have an idea as to what the transgression had been. Father Robert had been trying, in the name of God, to get him to confess to something that wasn't his fault. Totally his fault.

Realizing that he wasn't going to be able to sleep, Profitt had gotten out of bed, dressed, and started the day before the sun came up. He had requested that Klaus return to the city. He'd then sat, staring at the computer screen, realizing that no one was taking care of the funeral arrangements for Janet. Linda had been killed before she had finished the task.

He decided that he would call Rachel at home and tell her that she would now have to make the arrangements. There was no one else to do it.

Rachel answered the call, nodded when she saw her boss, and said, "I was arrested last night."

Profitt, who had been about to give her the assignment, stopped and said, "What?"

"The police came and arrested me, charging me with murdering Linda."

"Why didn't you call me? Immediately."

"They wouldn't allow it. They said I would be able to call once we got to the station. Then, suddenly, they changed their minds. Brought me home, apologized, and left."

"No," said Profitt, the anger burning through him. "That's simply not good enough. They have no right to break into homes and arrest people. I'll have Lupus look into this. A civil suit. Maybe criminal negligence."

"No," she said. "I'd rather just forget it."

Profitt nodded, and then asked, "Why didn't you call me last night?"

"Once I got back home, I figured it would wait until morning."

"Okay," said Profitt. "I want you to meet with Lupus this morning, giving him all the details including the names of every officer involved." He saw that she was about to protest and held up a hand. "No. You do this. If you decide you want to press forward, you'll have everything you need."

"Certainly," she said. "You called me."

"Yes." He seemed to be lost in thought. "I was hoping that you could come in early this morning. There are so many things that need to be done given what has happened."

She glanced off, at something that Profitt couldn't see. "About thirty minutes."

"Fine. I'll meet you in the office then." He reached out to disconnect and then stopped. "I can have Lupus meet us if you want."

"That can wait until this afternoon."

"Good. I'll see you in half an hour."

"Yes, sir."

Profitt disconnected and then moved away from the phone. He walked across the living room, opened the French doors, and stepped outside onto the balcony. The sun was bright and the air already hot and humid. It was going to be a miserable day for those who didn't have the luxuries of air-conditioning and tinted glass.

He looked over the railing, down into the street. It was still lost in shadows. It was daylight at the top of his building, and twilight a hundred or more stories below him. Cars moved on the streets, nearly invisible except for their headlights.

Unbidden thoughts of the night before came back to him. Father Robert pushing him for stories of his past, asking about the discovery of the mines and the riches and about the deaths of his partners. The priest had asked dozens of questions, pressing for as much information as he could get. Finally, the priest had labeled it a tragedy. A horrible tragedy, the father had said. To be so close to so much and lose it all.

Profitt turned and walked into the penthouse. He looked around and wondered what it would be like to be poor again. That was something that he could imagine because once he had been very poor. Once, to get through college, he'd had to work at a job that paid almost nothing with a boss who thought that he was Napoleon returned to Earth. A little man who thought that he controlled everyone's life because he ran the restaurant. A man who didn't understand that not everyone was afraid of him, or of losing a job.

The man had pushed too far and Profitt had nearly killed him with hot grease and a french fry basket. The man had spent more than a month in the hospital recuperating because even modern technology had trouble with third-degree burns. They'd nearly had to create a new category of burn because the grease had stuck to the flesh, eating its way to the bone and burning the bone itself.

Those who worked with him had said that there had been a problem with the machine, but everyone knew that Profitt had done it. Profitt had never returned to the job, but he had stayed in the city. Only once had he seen the man, on the street. Profitt had avoided him.

Now he felt just like he did in those hours after he'd attacked the man. He was waiting for the other shoe to fall, waiting for the police to come to get him, waiting for his life as he knew it to end.

He sat down on the couch and looked at the wineglasses that he and Father Robert had used the night before. None of the servants had come in yet so they hadn't picked them up.

"Everything that goes around comes around," Father Robert had warned. "Those who sinned will be punished for those sins unless they repent. God has set down the law since the beginning of time."

But Profitt had sat there and denied killing his wife or Linda Thoresson, sure that Father Robert believed him because it was the truth. He had told the priest that he didn't know what had happened. Or why it had happened. The problem was that Profitt was sure the priest wanted him to confess, if not to that, then something else.

Father Robert had left, saying, "I can't help you if you refuse to help yourself."

Profitt hadn't known what to say. He just opened the door and had said, "Thanks for coming."

He hoped it had been enough. Now, in the harsh light of day, having learned that Rachel had been arrested and accused of the crime, he wondered how long it would be before they came for him. A matter of hours, he was sure. For something that he hadn't done.

16 | Sometimes You Have to Make Your Own Breaks

Both OBrien and Ryan had decided that sitting in the hover car and watching a door that never opened was a waste of their time. Hughes had told them to find the ambassador and to follow him, but not to approach him. They had been told where to find him, and had driven to that spot, relieving the team that was in place there. Then they had sat quietly, through the remainder of the night, and waited for the ambassador to appear.

But the ambassador had not appeared. No one had appeared, except a priest, who walked down the street, turned into the office building, used a key to open the door, and disappeared inside. There had been no lights coming on, no evidence that the ambassador was there, nothing.

Finally, several hours after dawn, with the heat of the day building and with no cooling breeze from the sea, OBrien had tired of waiting. She'd mentioned it to Ryan, pointing out that they didn't know if the ambassador was, in fact, in the building they were watching.

"Hughes said he was. That patrol team we relieved said that he was."

"Yeah," countered OBrien, the sweat beading on her face, "but we don't know it for a fact."

"True," said Ryan, rolling down the window but finding that it did nothing to help.

"So," said OBrien, "we must establish that the subject is where we believe him to be. What if he surfaces in another part of the city while we sit here. You think that saying we'd taken over from another team but didn't see the ambassador for ourselves is going to cut it?"

Ryan pulled his sweat-damp shirt from his chest and blew down the front to try to cool himself. "I suppose not."

"Then we'll go up and ascertain that the subject is in the residence or office."

"We should," agreed Ryan reluctantly.

OBrien shoved open the hatch on her side of the hover car. She grabbed at the top and lifted herself clear, smoothing down her skirt as she stepped onto the street. It was slightly cooler outside, but not enough to make a difference.

The building in front of them was a low, three-story affair, with large windows on the ground floor, a glassed entryway, and some plantings, shrubs, bushes, and flowers along the walkway to the door.

OBrien and Ryan had been told that the entire ground floor was used by the ambassador as his office. The upper floors were his living area, set up along the same lines as those owned by Profitt. They were certainly getting to see how the other half lived.

"We knock on the door, or we just walk in?" asked Ryan.

"We just walk on in. Unless the door is locked," said OBrien. "Then, I guess we knock."

"And tell the ambassador what?"

She shrugged and then said, "Just ask a couple of routine questions. Once we know that he's inside, we'll just leave the house and return to the car."

"What about the priest?" said Ryan.

"What about him? We just say good morning to him and forget it."

They reached the front door and OBrien reached out, grabbing the handle. The door didn't budge. She looked around and found the intercom and bell. She pressed the button and waited.

"Yes."

"Ambassador?"

"Yes."

"Police."

"What do you want?"

OBrien glanced at Ryan and then at the tiny speaker by the door. "We'd like to talk to you."

"Please wait a moment. I will be right down."

"We should get out now," said Ryan. "We know that he's here."

"If we do that, he might be suspicious. Besides, we can confirm a couple of things from the other night. All completely routine and completely justified."

There was a buzz and OBrien pulled on the outer door. It opened. She entered, crossed to the second door, and found that it was unlocked. She pushed on through and was standing alone in a darkened hallway.

Ryan joined her a moment later. He stopped with his back to the wall, trying to watch both ways at once. He stood just behind OBrien, suddenly apprehensive, though he didn't know why.

A light appeared and a man stepped out. "Police?"

"Mr. Ambassador?" said OBrien.

"Sumner Gleason," he said, moving toward them, a hand out. He was wearing a robe, slippers, and little else. "I'm afraid that you got me out of the bath."

"I'm sorry, Mr. Ambassador," said OBrien. "We just needed to clear up a few things about the other night."

"Let's go upstairs. It'll be much more comfortable," said Gleason.

"Thank you," said OBrien.

Ryan said, "I think I'll remain down here, if that's all right."

Gleason shrugged. "If you prefer, though I have coffee and donuts upstairs."

"I'll wait," said Ryan.

OBrien shot him a glance, raising an eyebrow in question, but Ryan said nothing. The ambassador turned and walked back the way he'd come. As OBrien joined him, the door of an elevator opened.

He looked at her self-consciously and said, "A small luxury. I'm just fascinated with elevators."

They rode to the third floor and stepped off, into a large room that held little furniture and that seemed to orient toward a roof-top garden. Gleason held out a hand and said, "Let's sit by the doors."

"Do you own all this?" she asked.

"It belongs to me," said the ambassador. "I use the offices to conduct my business and live up here."

"Alone?"

They reached the table and Gleason pulled out the chair for her in a gesture that most had thought dead for two centuries. OBrien sat down, her back to the room, facing the open garden that was hidden from the street. It looked like they had lifted the roof from part of the building and created a jungle of trees, shrubs, bushes, and flowers. A short waterfall, no more than twelve feet high, splashed down into a reflecting pool that completed the picture.

"I find it relaxing," said Gleason. "But you wanted to know if I lived alone. Yes, I do. I know that it is obscene to spend so much indulging oneself when there are so many other ways the money could be used, but I did earn the money so I suppose I have the right to spend it."

"Certainly," said OBrien. Her attention was drawn to a bright green bird that dropped from a tree, opened its wings, and then swooped to a stop at the side of the pool. She turned toward him. "Ambassador? To what?"

He smiled. "The title, I'm afraid, is now honorary. At one time, I was ambassador to Altair. Now, I'm retired, living here and doing what I can for our poor planet."

"Alone?"

"Yes, I'm afraid so."

She turned to look into his eyes. "What about the priest?"

"What priest?" asked Gleason.

"My partner and I saw a priest enter this morning."

"Oh, Father Robert. Yes. A friend who sometimes stops by for a morning chat. He doesn't live here."

"He's still here?"

"No, he left," said Gleason.

"I didn't see him leave," said OBrien.

"Well, that may be, but he is gone." Grinning, Gleason waved a hand. "I invite you to search the premises, if that'll make you feel better."

"No, Mr. Ambassador, that's not necessary."

He waved a hand and said, "You're welcome to look." Then he lifted a pot from the center of the table, "Or if you'd rather, you could have some coffee."

"I'd be grateful."

Gleason pushed a cup at her and filled it. He then sat back in his chair and asked, "What did you want to ask me?"

OBrien sipped her coffee, put the cup down, and then pulled a notebook from her pocket. She made a show of flipping through it, pretended to read a blank page, and then asked, "What time did you get to Profitt's penthouse?"

"Oh, I don't remember, exactly. We had a dinner engagement and I was on time for that. Of course the police were there when I arrived."

"Did you see anyone suspicious?"

"No. I entered the lower level, saw the body and then one of your sergeants . . . you were there."

"Yes," said OBrien. "As I said, this is just routine." She made a note, took a sip of coffee. "Anything out of the ordinary there?"

Gleason was pensive and then said, "No. Not really. I was stunned when I learned the truth. Positively stunned."

OBrien finished her coffee. "Well, I thank you for your time. I hope, if we have more questions, that you won't mind if we stop back."

"No," said Gleason. "You might want to call first, just to ensure that I'm here."

"Thank you, Mr. Ambassador. I appreciate your kindness." She stuffed her notebook into a pocket.

"Let me show you out."

They walked to the elevator. When they stopped in front of it,

Gleason said, "You didn't have to come here to ask those questions. You already had the answers to them."

"We often reinterview . . . witnesses," said OBrien. "Sometimes they remember things that they forgot the first time."

"Did you learn?" asked Gleason as the doors opened.

"No."

She entered but he didn't. "Please come back," he said.

As the doors shut, she said, "Thank you."

On the ground floor, Ryan was standing right in front of the elevator as it opened. "You took your own sweet time about it."

"You should see that place up there. Doesn't look like much from down here, but it'd knock your socks off."

"He suspect anything?"

"Nope. Thinks it was all routine. Told me to come back if I had any other questions."

"He say anything about the priest?"

"Just that he's not here."

"The hell you say."

OBrien pointed at the front door and began to walk toward it. "Offered to let me search if I wanted. Couldn't see the point of it."

"No," said Ryan. "The priest isn't on our list of suspects anyway."

"That's what I thought."

Ryan opened the door and they stepped out into the heat of the morning. Traffic had picked up and the noise from the street washed out the other sounds. Ryan had to raise his voice. "If Gleason complains, we're going to catch hell."

"He's not going to complain. He gave me coffee and answered all my questions." She stopped at the curb and let two cars hover by. One had a defective flap, letting debris blow up and out, creating a dust cloud that followed it. She closed her eyes and turned her head to avoid the worst of it. "We could give him a ticket for that."

"If we wanted to waste our time chasing him down," said Ryan. "Let the boys and girls in Traffic do it."

They crossed the street and climbed into their car. OBrien

was behind the wheel. She twisted around, tugging at the hem of her skirt that had ridden up her thigh. Settled, she adjusted the seat back so that she could recline slightly, letting her look up, at the third floor of the building where she knew the garden was.

"So now we wait again," said Ryan. "With him knowing that the police are in the area."

"Were in the area," she corrected him.

"Hell, he's going to know that we're out here. The whole neighborhood is going to know it."

"Nothing we can do," said OBrien. She held a hand up to shield her eyes from the sun. The tint didn't cut the rays as well as it could. Upstairs, standing in a window of what she was sure was the garden area, she could see a shape. Gleason standing there watching her as she watched him. Sometimes police work was ridiculous.

17 | It's Not Exactly the Grassy Knoll

Brackett and his people were back in the tiny office assigned to them. Obo, as usual, was standing at the window, watching the people as they scrambled to work.

Brackett, holding on to the hard copy that had been spit out by the up-link, said, "It would seem to me that this Richard Holtz must have left some tracks. Either under his own name or under that of O'Shaughnessy."

"How hard could it be to sort through the hotel registrations?" asked Daily.

"Let's think this thing through carefully," said Brackett. "We know that Holtz is an off-worlder. That means he must have a base on this planet. Since he was in his O'Shaughnessy disguise when he was killed, it would mean that the room, base, whatever, was secured in another identity."

"Of course," said Daily.

"So we have to find him in that other identity," said Brackett. He grinned. "Now we need the locals. Sergeant Hughes and his people can help."

"You going to ask him?" asked Daily.

"Sure. I don't mind groveling in front of the locals. Makes for good public relations."

"Right," said Daily.

"Well," said Brackett, standing.

Before he could move, Hughes entered the office. "Good morning."

"You have any coffee?" asked Brackett.

"Coffee."

"I'm kidding," said Brackett. "Have a seat. Got a couple of questions for you."

Hughes began to turn red. A vein on his forehead began to throb. "You have questions for me. We've been working all night and you have questions."

"Let me rephrase that," said Brackett. "We've also been working and have a new direction to go and thought that we could work together on it."

Hughes relaxed visibly. "I'm sorry. I have been working all night. I've got people out to watch Gleason, Profitt, his secretary, and his house employees."

"Why Gleason?"

"Because I saw that clown standing over the body and no one has told me how he got into the hotel and into the penthouse without Profitt being alerted. He was there, right after the death of Janet Profitt, so we're watching him."

"Good," said Brackett. He pulled the hard copy closer and added, "We got this a few hours ago."

Hughes scanned it. "A professional assassin?"

"Makes me wonder if there isn't a connection between that incident and what happened later," said Brackett.

"Yeah," said Hughes.

"The question," said Brackett, "is whether or not we can check to see who is staying in the city. Tourists, visitors, that sort of thing."

"We don't have a central collection. I could have a couple of officers check it out. Take several hours."

"Here's my thinking," said Brackett. "Holtz must have had a base from which to operate. He might have used his real identity, but he might have used a false one in case we made his Holtz identity."

Daily spoke up. "Or is there some other place he could be staying?"

"There are houses that rent rooms by the day and week," said Hughes.

"Or," said Brackett, "I suppose he could have found a woman and paid her. No records at all."

"A thought occurs to me," said Hughes. "If he booked a room, regardless of the name he used, he's not going to be checking out. Someone might have filed a missing person's report."

"Good thought," said Brackett.

"I can check that out," said Hughes.

Brackett turned and leaned to the right. "Obo. Want tap into the computer system?"

"I be happy to do so," said Obo, sitting at the table. "You want I should look for missing persons."

"Yes."

Obo pulled the up-link around, sat for a moment, and began to type.

Brackett watched, and then stood, moving around so that he could watch the screen. For a moment nothing appeared and then the screen flashed, "No missing persons reported by hotel staff in the specified time frame."

Daily said, "Why not ask for the names of people who failed to check out."

Obo looked at her but didn't move to type. "I do not understand."

"Let me have that," said Daily. She pulled the keyboard around, thought about it, and then typed in the question.

Nothing appeared except for the blinking cursor. Then four names came up.

"Bingo," said Daily.

Brackett looked at them. One was a woman and he was going to discount it and then thought, Why not register in the name of a woman? A simple device that might buy some extra time if someone was searching.

"It can't be this easy," said Hughes.

"Sometimes you fall into it," said Brackett. "You stir around enough and something floats to the surface."

"How do you want to handle it?" asked Hughes.

"Hell," said Brackett, "let's just take them in alphabetical order."

"All of us?"

"We'll handle it," said Brackett.

Hughes sat for a moment and then said, "I can check with my field teams."

"Okay," said Brackett. "Obo, you want to stay here and coordinate?"

"Obo stay."

"Let's do it."

It was the third one on the list. Brackett had decided that it wasn't going to work. It had been a good idea that just hadn't worked out. Holtz wouldn't be so stupid as to rent a hotel room and if he did, they wouldn't be able to find it so easily.

The manager had packed up everything left in the room and stored it in the lower level so that it would be out of the way. "The only thing, don't take anything unless you tell me about it," he said.

There were four cardboard boxes, one on top of the other. A suitcase stood next to them. It looked as if it had been through a hundred different spaceports.

Brackett opened the top box. "Just clothes. Shirts, socks, and a leather belt."

He lifted the box, set it on the floor, and opened the second one. "Pants, underwear . . . and a notebook." He pulled it out and flipped through it. "Didn't write much down." He handed that to Daily.

He moved it out of the way and dug into the third one. Shaving gear, and a small black bag. Brackett opened it. "Theatrical makeup."

"Here's something," said Daily. "Address of the Star Rest Hotel."

"Meaningless by itself," said Brackett.

"Connects to the Star Rest."

"But we don't know this guy is Holtz."

Daily looked at him. "We've got the name of the hotel and you've got a case of theatrical makeup."

"Circumstantial so far." He moved the third box to the floor and dug into the fourth. He found a holo of Rama Lu O'Shaughnessy. He turned it around so that Daily could see it. "I think we've just gone beyond circumstantial."

Daily, who had been crouched, suddenly sat back, as if she'd just run completely out of energy. Her hands were shaking as the import of what they'd found sank in.

"We've got him . . ."

"Jennifer, the man is dead. We've had him for several days now."

"But it's all come together. We've linked Holtz to O'Shaughnessy and to the Star Rest Hotel."

"Yes," agreed Brackett, "but at the moment, it's a dead end."

She grinned at him and said, "What if I can give you another lead?"

"That would be helpful."

"There's a mention of a Club BelaDona and the singer there."

"Could be that he just dropped into the club for a drink."

"You're going to ignore that he mentions the club and the singer specifically?"

"No," said Brackett. "I just don't want you to get too excited about it. Could be a coincidence." He continued to dig through the last box, finding little of interest.

"Shouldn't the lab go through this stuff?" she asked.

"Yeah," said Brackett, nodding. He began to pack the fourth box. He closed it up. "We'll need to talk to the manager about this."

"Then we go to the last place on our list?"

"No. We'll give it to Hughes and let him check it out because we're going to the Club BelaDona."

Naturally, early in the morning, the club was closed. The mall was wide open, filled with people, but the club wasn't due to open again until late in the afternoon. Through one of the small, dark windows holding neon signs announcing beers that hadn't even been available on Earth for a century, Brackett could see one man moving around.

Daily pointed at the poster with a full-color holo of Lana Diamond in costume on the stage. "Well, this confirms that he was here recently."

Brackett pounded on the door and then looked through the window. He'd gotten the attention of the man inside who was now shaking his head, telling Brackett that they were closed.

Pulling his badge, he said to Daily, "Never fails to amaze me. You knock on the door and they tell you that they're closed. Like we couldn't figure that out for ourselves." He held the badge against the window, tapped on the glass, and waited for the man to look up again.

A moment later the door opened and the man, dressed in a dirty white T-shirt, a stained apron, faded blue jeans, and holding a mop, asked, "What do you want?"

Brackett flashed his badge again. "Police."

"I can see that."

Brackett moved to step by the man, but he blocked the way. Brackett could see a dark club, tables pushed to one side, chairs stacked on the tables. The floor was wet where the man had been mopping it.

"What do you want?"

Daily pointed at the poster again. "Lana Diamond. Where is she?"

"Not here. Why do you want her?"

Brackett smiled thinly. "Your questions are becoming tiresome. Let's do this. We'll ask and you respond. If you believe that it's too much trouble, we'll head to the precinct and you can tell the people there why you should retain your liquor license and the fire marshal will inspect your establishment to make sure that you're in compliance with the various codes."

The man let his mop drop and held out his wrists for the handcuffs. "Let's go talk to the man."

Brackett laughed. "Okay. You win that one. We need to talk

to Diamond about a man she might have seen here in the last few days."

Daily held out the photo of Holtz. "This man."

"Nope. I don't remember him being in here. But I get a thousand a night."

"He left indications that he'd been here and that he was interested in this singer."

"Means nothing. Lots of guys come in here and get the hots for Lana."

"I understand that," said Brackett. "We just want to talk to her about this man. She might remember something that could be of use to us."

"Come on in. I'll give you Lana's address, but you're just wasting your time."

"My time to waste," said Brackett.

The man led them through the club to a small room in the back that was barely big enough to contain the desk, file cabinet, and chair. On the wall over the desk was a window that looked out on the stage.

Pawing through a stack of cards, he held one up. "Address right here. Not a very good place to live, but cheap."

Daily moved forward and copied it down. "Thanks."

As they left, Daily said, "He's going to call her and let her know that we're on the way."

"Yeah, I thought of that, but then, we're not in a real hurry. If we miss her at her place, we can catch her here tonight."

"You're just looking for an excuse to come to the club," said Daily.

"You see," said Brackett, taking on the tone of a college professor, "when we have the opportunity to explore new worlds and to study the culture of those planets, we must take advantage of the opportunity."

"Not to mention that looking at naked women is fun," said Daily.

"Not fun," said Brackett. "Educational. Besides, there might be some naked men around here for you to look at."

"Sure," said Daily. "I believe that."

"Anyway," said Brackett as they reached the escalator, "she'll probably be at home and my excuse flies out the window."

"If she's there," said Daily.

"Yeah. If."

18 | On the Street Where You Live

OBrien was nearly asleep. She'd slipped down so that her knees were jammed against the dashboard and her head was on the back of the seat. It didn't look comfortable, but her eyes were closed and her breathing was regular.

Ryan, on the other hand, the sweat running down his face, was wide awake. The heat was making him edgy. Little sounds, the hum of other hover cars, a kid screaming in the distance, a dog barking, were enough to set him off. When he glanced at his partner, he wanted to punch her. It wasn't fair that she could sleep, while he had to sit there, his eyes on the building, waiting to see what Gleason did.

A man walked down the street, stopped, and looked right at Ryan, and then continued on. At the corner, he hesitated, glanced back, and finally disappeared.

Ryan turned his attention to the front of Gleason's building and saw the door open. Gleason was standing with his back to them, locking the door.

Ryan slapped OBrien on the shoulder. "He's on the move."

"What?" She sat up, rubbed her eyes, and then saw Gleason walking toward them. Without thinking, she ducked.

"There he goes," said Ryan.

Gleason was walking down the street. He didn't seem to care that anyone was watching him. In fact, he didn't act as if he knew it.

"Start the car," said Ryan.

OBrien fumbled with the keys, and then turned them. The engine coughed to life and the car came up, hovering on a cushion of air. She held it steady.

Gleason climbed into a car and it started. He rolled down the window, stuck his head out, and looked back at the approaching traffic. One car passed him and he pulled out, making a U-turn.

"There he goes," said Ryan.

"I see that," said OBrien. She eased forward, saw that nothing was in the way, and pulled out, but tried to stay a hundred yards behind Gleason.

"He's got to know we're here," said Ryan.

"Doesn't really matter."

A hover car pulled in between them. OBrien fell even farther back until they could just make out Gleason's car. It turned onto a side street. OBrien pulled up to the corner, slowed, and surveyed the street before she drove down it. Gleason was a block ahead of them.

"You're dropping back too far," said Ryan.

"I'm trying to avoid detection. He must have seen that other car turn off. Going to give him a false sense of security."

"He'll get real secure if you lose him."

"I'm not going to lose him."

"He's turning up there. Hurry up," said Ryan, pointing.

"I see what he's doing," said OBrien. "Relax." She accelerated and then slowed.

Gleason's car turned another corner then, as if trying to lose the tail. "See," said Ryan.

Now OBrien stepped on it. The engine roared, creating a thick cloud of dust that slipped under the fenders, obscuring the street to the sides of the car, but neither cared. They raced forward. As they reached the corner and turned, they saw that Gleason was two blocks ahead and seemed to be accelerating.

"We're blown," said OBrien.

"Doesn't matter," said Ryan. "Stick with him. Those are our orders."

Gleason turned again. When they reached the corner,

Gleason had slowed down and was glancing to the left, as if trying to see the numbers on the buildings.

"Hold it," said Ryan.

They stopped in the intersection. "What in the hell is he doing?"

"Looking for something," said OBrien.

"Hold it here," he said, watching as Gleason slowed nearly to a stop.

Gleason pulled to the side of the street and stopped. He shut down his car and then climbed out.

"Pull ahead," said Ryan. "To the curb."

As they did, Gleason looked back up the street, as if searching for those who had been behind him. Satisfied that he was alone, he hurried across the street, toward a two-story, dilapidated building.

"Back up," said Ryan.

"Give me a chance here." She backed up, turned, and started down the street.

"Find a place to park," said Ryan. "Not too close to his car."

"How about here?"

"Fine."

OBrien pulled to the curb. She stopped the car and shut down the engine. The hover car settled, rocking right and then left. As it stabilized, Ryan pushed open his door. "I'll check this out. You wait here. If he comes out and starts to drive off, you follow him. I'll catch another ride later."

"Understood."

Ryan hurried around the rear of the hover car, stopped to check the traffic, and then walked to the opposite curb. He walked on down the street, spotted the house that he thought Gleason had entered, and glanced at the number. There was nothing unusual about it.

He continued on, looking at the sides. A residence, maybe with rooms to rent. A side yard filled with bushes with trash, boxes, cans, and bottles thrown under them.

He walked on down to the corner, and then stopped, looking back. Gleason's car was parked opposite. He walked to it and peeked in the window. Nothing visible on the seats or on the floor.

Turning, he moved back to the sidewalk. For a moment he stood, staring at the building, wondering if they should go on in.

He strolled along, stopping at the intersection with the walkway that led to the front door. He looked up at the building, trying to see anything through the windows. But it was dark inside and the sunlight was wrong. He could see nothing.

He continued on, walking back to the hover car. He opened the door and climbed in.

"Well?"

"Hell, I don't know. Can't see any reason for an ambassador to come here."

"So what do we do?"

"We sit here and watch, just as we've been told to do."

Brackett finally pulled to the curb and said, "You were supposed to be the navigator. You've got the map."

"But you made the wrong turn."

"You told me to turn. I don't know where the street is. I was listening to you."

Daily turned the map around so that the bottom was at the top and then asked, "What was that last cross street?"

"Hillsboro."

"Hillsboro. Hillsboro? Ah. And we're on?"

"Buckholtz."

"Okay, that means we're right here. Now, if we continue on here for two or three blocks and then turn . . . right. We should connect."

"Right on what?"

"Maximillian."

"Okay." Brackett pulled away from the curb, ducked his head to read the street sign, and drove on. He found Maximillian and turned to the right. "What's the next cross street?"

"Nicollete."

They passed the sign. "Right. Okay. We're on track again."

"See. We're not lost."

"Okay," said Brackett, laughing. "And if we were lost, we've found our way back."

Brackett followed the directions, made the turns, and then asked, "What was the number?"

"You know, if I wasn't here, I don't think you'd be able to get anywhere."

"Nope," said Brackett, "I'd just work with a local who knew his way around."

"Or hers."

"Whatever."

Daily ducked, read a couple of numbers. "If they follow the system used on other planets, it should be in the next block."

They drove on for a moment, slowly, taking in the neighborhood, getting the feel of it. The buildings, houses, and apartments, the yards and debris stored in them, told both Brackett and Daily something about the people who lived there.

Daily pointed suddenly and said, "Right there."

Brackett searched for a parking place and then said, "That a police vehicle?"

"Where?" She turned and said, "That looks like Hughes's two young officers."

"Now what in the hell are they doing here?"

"Looks like some kind of stakeout."

Brackett drove on by the apartment house and continued down the street. He turned the corner, drove about halfway down, and then stopped. "Now that's very strange."

Daily understood what was going on. She knew that they couldn't stop on the same block. Two cop cars would be obvious to everyone within ten blocks.

"This is an interesting coincidence," said Daily.

"Very." Brackett rubbed his cheek. A woman walked by the car but paid no attention to them. "I'm going to walk by and see what I can find out." He turned in his seat but couldn't see back to the apartment.

"I stay here," said Daily.

"And monitor the radio. Study the map. Watch the street."

"Thanks, Loot. I appreciate it."

Brackett climbed out, took off his jacket, and tossed it into the car. He took off his sunglasses to wipe them, but the sun was so bright, he couldn't stand it. Leaning down, looking into the car at Daily, he said, "I'll be back in about ten, fifteen minutes."

"Sure."

Brackett walked down the street, turned the corner, and headed toward the parked police car. He watched the two people in it, waiting for one of them to spot him, but their attention was focused on the house across the street.

Ryan looked up suddenly, spotted Brackett, and sat for a moment, looking like he'd seen a ghost. He said something to OBrien and then opened the door, climbing out.

Brackett kept walking, but as he approached Ryan, he said, "Walk with me for a moment."

"Sure. What's going on here?"

"I was going to ask you the same question," said Brackett.

Ryan hesitated for a moment and then said, "We were assigned to watch Ambassador Gleason. He left his residence and drove here. He went inside and hasn't come out."

Brackett stopped walking and looked at the young police officer. "Gleason is here?" He turned and looked at the house where Lana Diamond was supposed to live. "Where?"

Ryan started to point.

"No!" yelled Brackett. "What number?"

Ryan told him.

"Gleason is in there?" He turned and studied the house again. "I come over to talk to a woman who might have been involved with the man who was killed in the Star Rest. Now, you're here following one of the three men that was in Profitt's apartment within hours of finding the body of Janet Profitt."

"Do you believe in coincidence?" asked Ryan.

"Not like this," said Brackett. "There is no way to believe that this is a coincidence." He stared at the house.

"We've been told to watch Gleason," said Ryan.

"And I want to talk to Lana Diamond. Okay. You continue to watch and I'll go in with my partner. The odds are that Gleason is not in with Lana Diamond."

"But what are the odds that Gleason would lead us to the street where she lives and walk into the building where she lives?" asked Ryan.

"And what are the odds that the two people we follow would have been in the Star Rest on the day that another two people were killed?" asked Brackett. "Okay. You get back into your car and continue your surveillance. We'll go talk to Diamond and see what happens."

"Sure, Loot."

Brackett turned and started back toward his car. In the pit of his stomach, he felt that they were on to something. The problem was, he didn't know what it was.

19 | An Infinite Number of Monkeys . . .

Hughes stood just outside the doors that led into the offices of Profitt's investment corporation and philanthropic foundation. The hallway had widened until it was like a waiting room complete with a couch, a couple of chairs, a table holding magazines, and a telephone. A button camera was mounted above the doors, set on a swivel so that it could see into all areas of the area.

Hughes pulled his wallet and badge from his hip pocket and held it up so that the button camera would have no trouble spotting it. He didn't say a word, didn't knock, and didn't use the phone. After a minute, the doors opened and Rachel de vo Willom appeared.

"Sergeant?"

"I have some questions that I need to ask. And I would like to see Mr. Profitt."

"Mr. Profitt is not seeing anyone today. He is in mourning over the death of his wife and one of his close associates."

"Yes," said Hughes. "Well, I'm afraid that this is a little more than a social or business visit. Let's say that it is official and that I'll see him one way or another."

"I assume that you have a warrant," she said, her voice hardening.

"With me? No. But I can get one, if that's necessary, and then I won't be in a good mood. It's so much easier if you and Mr. Profitt cooperate."

"Please wait here," she said finally. She retreated a step and closed the doors.

Hughes thought that he had been abandoned. He considered leaving, going to find a friendly judge who wasn't so frightened of the power that Profitt had that he would sign an order so that Hughes could penetrate the inner sanctum of Profitt's empire.

But Rachel opened the doors again and stepped back, out of the way. "Please come with me."

"Thank you."

She led him through a short corridor that looked as if it could hide a dozen places for men with weapons and into a large office. She continued across it and stopped at another set of double doors. She knocked and then opened them. "Go on in."

Hughes did as he was told, prepared to see the great man again. He stopped just inside.

"What in the hell do you mean by arresting my secretary?" demanded Profitt.

"I . . ."

"And what do you mean by coming here with high-handed threats of legal action? I must warn you that I've called my attorney and he is on his way down here."

"Mr. Profitt," said Hughes, "we arrested your secretary based on forensic evidence developed at the 107th . . ."

"What the hell is the 107th?"

Hughes took a step forward, glanced at the chairs, but didn't move toward them. "The 107th is the Star Precinct that you demanded . . ."

"Okay."

"They developed evidence that linked your secretary to the crimes in . . . I guess a generous assessment would be to say a preliminary way. As they continued to work, she was then eliminated as a suspect."

"I don't like the way you jumped the gun and arrested her."

Hughes grinned and said, "Well, there again, that is what happens when you deal with outsiders. They don't understand the nuances of our planet."

Profitt relaxed slightly. He pointed at one of the chairs. "Why don't you sit down."

"Thank you." Hughes did as he was told and then crossed his legs, setting an ankle on his knee. He picked at the lint of his sock. "We got that straightened out. But then, you're partly to blame."

"How so?"

"You're the one who said that you saw her running from the apartment. Given the forensic evidence, what conclusion did you expect us to draw?"

Profitt sank into his chair. "I told your officer, what's her name, that I wasn't sure and that when I called down here, Rachel was at her desk."

"Whatever," said Hughes, waving a hand.

"What can I do for you?" asked Profitt.

"Well," said Hughes, "I'm not sure."

"I'm a busy man," said Profitt. "I don't like to waste time and I don't like to have people waste it for me."

Hughes took out his notebook and a pen. He flipped the notebook open and then said, "I wanted to get a feel for your background."

"I can have my secretary give you a very good book that covers all that in depth."

"Yes, sir, I'm sure she could, but then you miss the nuances. I wanted to hear you talk about it."

"Maybe some other time," said Profitt.

Hughes didn't budge and didn't speak. He stared at Profitt, waiting.

"A few minutes," said Profitt. "As long as my attorney is present."

Hughes shrugged. "Why do you need an attorney? We're going to be talking about ancient history here. Not the crimes that have been committed in the last few days."

"Am I a suspect?" asked Profitt.

"Now there's an interesting question," said Hughes. "The spouse is always a suspect because the spouse is guilty in a large number of cases. And friends are suspects because, in most cases, the victim knew the killer. There are very few murders committed where the victim and the killer are total strangers. So, to answer your question, statistically, you are a suspect."

"That doesn't answer the question, Sergeant," said Profitt. "What do you think?"

"I think that there is a chance that you killed your wife and that Linda Thoresson said something to you that made you think that she knew too much about it so you killed her."

"How did I get out of the locked room?"

"You bribed your employee, Klaus, to corroborate your story."

"Then I am at the mercy of Klaus."

Hughes nodded. "But he is an accomplice, if you did kill her, so that you have some hold over him."

"I suppose," said Profitt. "So, you think I did it."

"No," said Hughes. "I never said that. I said that you were a suspect. However, I don't think you did it."

"Thank you for that," said Profitt. "But I still want my attorney present."

"Whatever."

Profitt reached out and touched a button. The door opened and a man dressed in a gray suit entered. He nodded at Profitt but didn't speak. He took a seat on the couch and never said a word.

"Okay. What do you want to know?" asked Profitt.

"When you started out, there were three of you."

"So long ago," said Profitt. "Yes. There were three of us. Jason Argon, David Kincaid, and me. Pooled our resources and took off to make our fortune."

He laughed once. A single bark. "Youth . . . we were sure that we would all become rich. Three friends who flew off into space, landing on planets that were less than hospitable. Planets that were so cold that you would freeze solid in a matter of seconds. Planets where the atmosphere was poisonous. Worlds that we stayed on just long enough to prepare to get off. Worlds where the sky was dark and the wind blew all the time. Always searching for something valuable enough to force Earth to take notice. Looking for a world of wealth.

"We found it here. The planet was rougher then. No people. Just the thick jungle over half of the planet. Big catlike creatures that preyed on everything else. Birds and lizards. Strange creatures, some of them with deadly bites."

"What happened to your friends?"

Profitt ignored the question. "It was the iridium. Needed for the star drives. Without it, we couldn't travel among the stars. Here, it was everywhere. More than enough to make it worthwhile for the expense of mining it and refining it and bringing in the people to do it.

"The iridium was everywhere here. No one had to dig it out of deep holes. Scrape the ground with earth-moving equipment, push it into the hoppers, and in a day, two days, you had a mountain of iridium. More than enough to fuel every starship ever built or that we can possibly build in the next ten years. Everything that we need. Or needed."

Profitt stopped talking and then looked up at the ceiling, as if studying something there.

"What happened to your friends?" asked Hughes again.

"You don't have to answer that," said the attorney.

"It doesn't matter," said Profitt. "They were killed. Some kind of creature killed Argon. Killed him and dragged his body off. I never did find it. The body, I mean."

"And the other man?"

"Radiation killed him. Got sick and died in about four hours. Just wasted away in front of my eyes."

"How do you know if Argon is dead?" asked Hughes.

"Oh, I saw the beast that got him. It had ripped him open. There was blood all over his belly. I could see bone. But I couldn't get to him. No way I could get to him."

"What happened to Kincaid's body?"

"I buried it. I was sick too, but I buried it. Dug the grave at the foot of a tree, figuring I could find it again, but I never did. Both my friends. Dead."

"You registered their deaths?" asked Hughes.

"When I was back. Police went over the computer logs and the various . . ."

"Mr. Profitt," said Lupus, "I don't think you need to go into that area. It's all been documented to the satisfaction of the various police agencies."

Profitt shrugged. He looked at Hughes and waited for the next question.

"The bodies were gone," said Hughes.

"You're not suggesting that either Kincaid or Argon survived, are you?"

"No. I was merely making a comment."

Lupus spoke up again. "I'm afraid that I don't see the relevance of this line of questioning. Not with the recent deaths."

"That was something that I wanted to get into," said Hughes. "Do you know anyone named Richard Holtz?"

Profitt was quiet for a moment. "Name means nothing to me."

"He was the man that was killed here."

"I thought that Rama Lu O'Shaughnessy was the name of the man."

"Cover identity," said Hughes. "You know any reason why someone would want to kill you?"

"Mr. Hughes," said Lupus.

"Sergeant."

"Sergeant Hughes, a man in Mr. Profitt's position has enemies. Can't be helped. There are those who feel that Mr. Profitt owes them something. They come begging for money and when it is denied, they believe that Mr. Profitt should die. They believe that he is part of a conspiracy to keep them in the dirt. All sorts of fanciful things. People who think that Mr. Profitt owes them. People who have never contacted us."

"I suppose," said Hughes. He turned his attention on Profitt and sat, waiting.

"I've wished that there was something I could have done to

save my friends. I've always wished that. But the beast had killed Jason before I had a chance to do a thing."

"Do you think your secretary could be the killer?"

"Rachel? I thought you had eliminated her as a suspect."

"She was still in the area when Thoresson was killed."

"No," said Profitt. "I don't think she had a thing to do with it."

"Any connection between your wife and Linda Thoresson?"

"I think they might have met once. Thoresson was an employee."

"What was she doing up in your apartment?"

Lupus said, "You don't have to answer that."

"She was gathering the clothing to be used to bury my wife. As a private secretary, her job was to do whatever I assigned her to do. Selecting that clothing was a task I assigned."

Hughes closed his notebook. He shook his head slowly. "I just don't see anything here that would result in the deaths of three people."

"Two," said Lupus.

"No," said Hughes. "We're concerned with the death of Holtz too."

Lupus nodded. "Of course."

"Do you have any theories?" asked Profitt. "Any reasons for that?"

"There is nothing that makes sense. It would seem that Holtz was after you, but then, your wife was killed only a short time later. That would suggest that she was the target. But why would anyone want to kill her? She didn't have the money or the power. You're the only target that makes sense. As I say, nothing that makes any sense."

"If there is anything that I can do to assist you, please contact us. I'll tell Rachel to add your name to the list of those who can get right to me."

Hughes realized that he had been dismissed. He wondered when he had lost control. Profitt had answered the questions and then decided that it was time for Hughes to leave. For the moment, he waited, but the interview was over. There wasn't anything else that he wanted to ask.

"Thank you for your time."

Profitt stood and held out his hand. "Please find out who killed my wife."

"We're trying."

20 | How Do They Do That?

Brackett, standing on the curb and looking down into the car, told Daily, "We're going in."

"And what about Gleason?"

"There is no reason to assume that Gleason will be in the same place. It's a rooming house."

"You think that it's a coincidence," said Daily. She had one hand up to shield her eyes from the brightness of the morning sun.

"I don't think anything at the moment," he said. "We've a legitimate reason to be here. If we find Gleason, we just ignore it for the moment. If we don't see him, then there is nothing to worry about."

Daily nodded and opened the door. She climbed out and then surveyed the block. "Crummy neighborhood. Why would an ambassador, even a retired ambassador, want to come here?"

"Maybe he's hot for Diamond."

"A vidjournalist's dream. Former high-ranking official caught in 'Love Nest with Torch Singer.' "

Brackett laughed. "I think you've been reading too much of your own fiction."

"Be one hell of an interesting twist."

"No one would believe it," said Brackett.

"Yet here we stand."

Brackett turned and began to walk off. "Let's get going and forget about your novel."

"I'm taking notes all the way," said Daily. "You never know what life experiences you can interject into a story. That guy this morning, that club owner or whatever he was. Perfect little scene."

They reached the corner, stopped, and then crossed the street. Brackett asked, "Where do you get the names of the people for your stories?"

"That's the hardest part. Finding names that seem to go together without sounding fake. Can't put a Cynthia together with a Hernandez."

"Why?"

"Well . . ."

"I think Cynthia Hernandez is a good name. One that you would remember. Not something you'd see on a tombstone and then forget."

Now Daily laughed. "A tombstone name. I'll have to remember that." As they turned to walk up to the rooming house, she asked, "How are we going to handle this?"

"Just flash the badge and ask the questions. Maybe show her the picture."

"You don't think she was involved then," said Daily.

"I don't believe I said that. She could be up to her eyebrows. I don't think it's likely, but now, with Gleason close at hand, I don't know what to think."

They entered and stopped in the entrance. A young man who looked to be six feet tall but couldn't have weighed more than a hundred twenty pounds appeared and asked, "How may I be of service?"

"Lana Diamond." Brackett pulled out his badge and showed it to the man.

"She in trouble?"

"No. Just routine. Might have seen something that will be useful to us."

"Upstairs. Room nineteen. On the left."

"Thanks."

Brackett and Daily climbed the stairs, listening to the pop of the ancient wood. He had the feeling that the house was a hundred years old, but knew it couldn't have been. Human pioneers hadn't settled the planet until twenty or thirty years earlier. Everything was built after that point.

At the top of the stairs, Brackett had the urge to pull his weapon. He touched his side, felt the pistol, and then unbuttoned his light jacket so that he'd be able to draw quickly, if he had to.

"Down here," said Daily.

They located the door, and then separated, one on either side of it. Brackett reached out and knocked. Waited, and knocked again.

"Yes?"

"Police."

"Just a moment." The door opened then and Lana Diamond stood there. "Yes?"

Brackett flashed his badge and ID and asked, "Mind if we come in?"

"It's the middle of the night," she said.

"It's the middle of the morning," said Daily.

"When you work all night, the morning becomes the middle of the night."

"Of course," said Brackett, nodding. "Just a couple of questions."

Diamond stepped back. Out of the way. Brackett entered and noticed the open wardrobe with men's clothes hanging in it. And he noticed that the bed hadn't been slept in. There were men's shoes sitting on the floor near it, and men's clothes draped over a chair, but no sign of the clothes that she had worn. There was an unnatural feel to the room, as if something was missing from it.

Daily pulled the picture out of her pocket and asked, "You know this man?"

Diamond barely looked at it and then shook her head. "Never seen him."

Brackett focused his attention on her. "We found your name in his personal effects. Thought maybe you could remember where you'd seen him."

"Nope."

"Look at the picture," said Daily. "We know that he was in the club."

"Lots of people come into the club. A thousand of them a night. I'm up on the stage, behind the lights. I rarely see them."

"You don't live alone," said Brackett.

"What makes you say that?"

"All the men's clothing," said Brackett. "Is your roommate here?"

"I have no roommate," said Diamond, turning to glance at the wardrobe. "I'm storing that for a friend. Until he gets on his feet."

"Sure," said Brackett. He turned his attention back to Diamond. "Where are the clothes that you wore?"

"What?"

"I see a man's suit looking as if it was just worn." He pointed to the chair. "I see shoes that look as if they were just removed, but I don't see anything that belongs to you. Nothing that you might have worn."

"What are you driving at?" asked Diamond.

For a moment Brackett said nothing. He just stood, looking at the room, and then said, "I don't know." He waited for Diamond to speak.

Finally, Daily asked, "You don't remember seeing this man around the club?"

"No. Not at all." Diamond looked from Daily to Brackett, as if watching a high-speed tennis match. "I don't remember him at all."

Brackett interrupted the interrogation suddenly. "Okay. Thanks." To Daily he said, "Let's get going so that she can get some sleep."

Daily shrugged.

Brackett moved to the door, turned, and said, "Thanks for your help. If you think of anything, let us know. Sergeant Hughes at the station house."

"Certainly."

They stepped into the hallway, and as the door closed, Daily asked, "What the hell was that all about?"

"The ambassador was in there somewhere."

"How do you know?"

"I looked at the clothes closely. Fine clothes. Well tailored that cost a bundle not all that long ago. Not the kind of thing that you leave with a friend as you look for a new apartment. I'll bet you big dough that the description of what the ambassador was wearing will match what we saw lying on that chair."

"So what?"

"I don't know," said Brackett. "But when two people that we're interested in show up in the same room, I get suspicious. Real suspicious."

Diamond wasn't happy. Police kept showing up at her apartment or club and asking questions. Too many police and too many questions. She moved around the room, touching things, as if to assure herself that they were real. She finally sat on the edge of the bed and looked at the suit. That had been the mistake. When the police announced themselves, she should have tossed it under the bed. And closed the wardrobe. Stupid. Stupid. Stupid.

And this place was burned. She should never have given the real address to Osbourne at the club. She should have known that he'd spill his guts the first time the police questioned him, but then, she hadn't known that Holtz would be so stupid as to write down her name.

"Idiot," she said, not sure if she meant herself or Holtz. But that was what happened when amateurs were brought in, even those who were highly recommended. Holtz had gotten himself killed by a robot. "Idiot," she repeated.

The Diamond identity was burned. The police knew about it. Knew where she lived. She'd have to dump it, which was too bad because she enjoyed the role. So many people so completely fooled. That was what had made it fun.

She looked around the room but there was nothing in it that she wanted to kept. In fact, anything she did keep could eventually come back to haunt her. Someone, someday, might recognize it, and that would be a path that would lead right back to her.

No, the only intelligent thing was to abandon everything that belonged to the Diamond identity. Leave it behind like a snake that abandons its skin as it grows and moves on. Shed the identity completely and totally.

She looked out the window, at the bright morning filled with building thunderheads, and decided that she'd better get out quickly. Before the police returned and asked questions that she couldn't answer.

Now it was Ryan who was on the verge of sleep and OBrien who was wide awake. She watched Brackett and Daily enter the rooming house, and fifteen or twenty minutes later watched them leave it. Neither looked in her direction, pretending as if she weren't there.

Ryan slipped down in the seat, his head resting against the door. He snored softly, making a little popping sound with his mouth as he exhaled. At first, OBrien didn't care. It didn't bother her. But the longer he kept it up, the more annoying it became. She reached over, pushed on his shoulder, and Ryan shifted around and was quiet.

She turned back to the rooming house and saw Gleason exit, walking quickly. Without a word to Ryan, she switched on the engine.

"What?"

"Our boy's on the move," she said.

Ryan was sitting upright, rubbing at his eyes with the heels of his hands, trying to focus. He stared out the window. "Where's Brackett?"

"He and Daily left about ten minutes ago."

Gleason had reached his vehicle and climbed in without looking to see if anyone was close. He started up, pulled out, and headed up the street.

"We want to stay close?" asked OBrien.

"Let's give him some space. Let him think that he's free and clear."

OBrien pulled out and kept her distance. With more traffic on the street now, it was easier to follow Gleason without being seen.

They made one turn and drove down a long street. There were single family houses along it. Small, compact houses created from plastic and metal, sucked out of the ground by fabrication machines.

Gleason made another turn but he wasn't trying to lose anyone. He was driving along, slowly, but not heading toward his own house.

"Where now?" asked Ryan.

"Just keep the log," said OBrien.

Gleason slowed and then turned into a parking lot. OBrien found a place on the street, where they could see Gleason and his car.

Gleason got out, looked around, as if wondering if anyone was following him, and then walked to another car. He opened it, and climbed in.

"Now, what the hell?" asked OBrien.

"Pretty crummy car for him," said Ryan.

Gleason started up, pulled out, and then slid to the street. He came back the way he'd come, passing OBrien and Ryan, who ducked down, as if that would fool anyone.

"Now this makes me suspicious," said Ryan. "The innocent do not switch vehicles that way."

"Could be a logical reason for it." She made a quick U-turn and fell in behind Gleason. It still looked as if the man had yet to spot them. Or it could be that he just didn't care.

They drove along, made two turns, and then Gleason stopped near a church. He got out and walked around to the rear of it, disappearing.

"Father Robert Hanssen, Pastor," said Ryan, reading the sign out front.

"This is getting interesting," said OBrien.

"Very."

21 | Would You Believe . . . the Butler?

The heat of the morning increased as the sun climbed higher. The landscape took on the appearance of a bad video, the colors all washed out by the brightness around them. Heat shimmered on the sidewalk and parking lot and baked the cars. Both OBrien and Ryan began to sweat.

OBrien reached out to the key.

"We start the engine to run the air-conditioning," said Ryan, "and we'll burn it up."

"We sit here much longer and we're going to burn up."

"Someone's coming," said Ryan, pointing.

"That's the priest."

"Think we should follow him?" asked Ryan.

"Our assignment is Gleason."

The priest walked into the parking lot and turned slowly, as if searching for anyone who might be watching. As he looked at their car, both OBrien and Ryan ducked.

"You think he saw us?"

"No," said Ryan.

OBrien peeked up and saw the priest standing at the door of Gleason's car. He opened it and climbed inside, behind the wheel.

"Now that's curious," said OBrien.

"It could explain Gleason's behavior. It was the priest's car and he was bringing it over."

"No," said OBrien. "Why would Gleason do that himself?

And where is he? He'd need the priest to give him a ride back to his car."

"True."

The priest had started the car and pulled to the street. There he hesitated as the traffic appeared and rolled past him quickly.

"We follow?" asked OBrien. "Now that he's in Gleason's car?"

"No," said Ryan. "Our assignment is the man and not the vehicle. We stay here."

The priest exited the parking lot and turned away, driving up the street rapidly. In seconds the car had disappeared from sight. OBrien and Ryan were still sitting in the hot car, sweating, and wishing that Gleason would come out so that they could get on with it.

"Maybe we should go into the church and see what he's doing," said OBrien.

"We already went into his house. We go in there and he could call the chief accusing us of harassment. He can't get out without us seeing it."

"Then maybe one of us could go get something cold to drink while the other watches."

"And then Gleason appears so that you drive off. If something happens to you, then I've got to explain why I left you alone."

"So we sit here and fry," said OBrien.

"Actually, I think what we're doing is baking."

As they drove back to the station, Brackett said, "That about does it. There's nothing else that we can do."

Daily was sitting so that she could lean her head against the headrest, her eyes closed against the glare of the morning sun. "Maybe there is something in Holtz's things that we overlooked. We didn't exactly go through them with a fine-tooth comb."

"No," agreed Brackett. He slowed down for the cross traffic and then accelerated across the street. "Still, we've a connection between Diamond and Holtz. That's something that should be explored."

"Not to mention," said Daily, her eyes still closed, "that we've got Gleason involved in this somehow. He was at that rooming house."

"I'll be willing to bet that we'd find that a few of the women are turning tricks out of it. That might be the connection."

"Gleason is using prostitutes?"

"Maybe," said Brackett. "There are men who find the power they have over the prostitute erotic. They know the prostitute's mission is to make them happy."

"I don't like it," said Daily. "Too easy. We've got two people, involved in the deaths at Profitt's penthouse at the same place."

"I know what you mean," said Brackett. He slowed and turned into the parking garage under the police building. They drove deeper, until Brackett found a place to park.

Daily sat up and opened her eyes. "So what are we going to do now?"

"I'm going to find Obo and tap into the mainframe at the 107th. Plug all this into the computer and see if it can draw any conclusions."

"What do you want me to do?" asked Daily.

"Probably get with Hughes and see what he knows. Maybe check on the background of Diamond. I'd be surprised if she was as innocent as she pretends to be."

"You think she had something to do with the murders?"

"I don't like the way her name turned up in the belongings of the assassin. Until we know a little more about her, I want her kept on the list of suspects."

Daily reached up and scratched the top of her head, her long fingernails making a whispering sound against her scalp. "That's not getting us any closer to who killed Janet Profitt."

"We don't know that," said Brackett. "At the moment, we don't know anything for certain."

Daily reached over and opened her side of the hover car but she didn't get out. "You think the locals are protecting Profitt because of what he's done for them?"

"I wouldn't put it past them, but then, there is no evidence of it."

"So we just continue to march?"

"Not much else we can do."

Father Robert Hanssen drove to the penthouse headquarters of Profitt. He had no trouble parking the car, taking a strip of sidewalk with a red curb that was designated for emergency vehicles. If the police had asked, he would have told him that he was there to meet with one of his congregation who had experienced a personal tragedy and had that not worked, he would have dropped Profitt's name.

But the police didn't find him and quiz him. The doorman opened the door and let him into the hotel lobby. Father Robert walked across the marble expanse, to the private elevators that led up into Profitt's domain.

He rode up, quickly, looking into the mirror that was the back wall, studying his image carefully. Every hair was in place. His clothes, though old and getting a little threadbare, were clean and pressed. He looked the role of the country priest coming to call on his grieving parishioner.

The elevator stopped and the door opened onto the entrance. He stepped out, into the wide hallway, and as he started across it, the double doors at the far end opened. Rachel appeared and said, "Father Robert."

"Hello, my dear. How is our friend?"

She shrugged. "Well, I guess. The situation, with the police and the murder is very stressful."

"Yes, I suppose it is. Do you think that he'll have time to see me?"

Rachel stepped back, out of the way. "I know that Mr. Profitt wants to see you." She grinned. "Yours is one of the few names on his list."

"I hope that I'm able to bring some comfort." He passed through the doors.

Rachel closed them and walked to her desk. "Let me announce you." She pushed a button and said, "Father Robert is here."

An instant later Profitt appeared at the door of his office. He held out a hand to be shaken and said, "Father Robert. I was going to call you this afternoon."

Hanssen walked by Profitt and into the interior of the large, plush office. He fell to his knees in front of the desk, looking beyond it, through the windows that gave a view of the shallow sea in the distance.

"Shall we pray together?" asked the priest.

Profitt stood at the door for a moment, looking, then closed the door and walked to the priest. He got to his knees, clasped his hands together, and said, "Yes, Father."

The priest turned his face up, looking into the sky, and said, "Heavenly Father, Who has brought us to this point, we beseech You for guidance."

For five minutes, Father Robert spoke out loud, his eyes now closed. He asked for help, for forgiveness, for strength to endure the trials of the coming days and weeks. He prayed in a voice that rose as he lost himself in the task. He nearly screamed the last few words, and then fell silent, drained. Finally he climbed to his feet.

"You may stand, my son."

Profitt got up, looked at the priest, and said simply, "Thank you, Father." He walked to his desk, was about to sit in the chair behind it, and then changed his mind. Instead, he took one of the two visitor's chairs near the couch.

The priest sat down on the couch and carefully crossed his legs. He glanced to the right, where there was a door that led into the office. "I think that we should be alone."

Profitt understood immediately. He locked both doors into the office and then leaned over his desk. Using the intercom, he said, "Rachel, I don't want to be disturbed for the rest of the afternoon."

"We have Jenkins coming in this afternoon. You've already postponed him twice."

"Please call him and explain the situation. Besides, he wants money from me, so he'll take the postponement with good spirits, even if he's enormously annoyed."

"Certainly, Mr. Profitt."

Turning to the priest, Profitt said, "Now we won't be disturbed until we're ready."

"That's good," said Hanssen.

Profitt sat down and didn't speak right away. It was almost as if he were a small boy with a big problem and didn't know how to talk about it. He took a deep breath, sighed, and said, "I don't understand why this is happening to me."

"It is the way of the universe," said Father Robert. "We often don't understand that which is happening to us until it is too late for us to do a thing about it."

"But Janet didn't deserve to die like that."

"It was quick and painless," said the priest. "She didn't suffer."

Profitt didn't notice that the priest was talking as if he had been there when Janet had died. Instead, he said, "I hope that is right."

"Those who are closest to us," said the priest, "sometimes know the least about us. Sometimes they suffer for the things that we have done."

Profitt nodded dumbly and thought back to a time when the planet was untamed and savage. Of three friends in a broken-down ship braving the rigors of space to find fortune. Of betrayal and death on a planet dozens of light-years from home. The images flared in his mind, unbidden, as if they provided a clue about the death of his wife and the death of his private secretary.

"You have sinned, my son."

"Of course," replied Profitt. "We all have. We all do."

"But some sins are worse than others. Some people sin more than others."

"I've tried to be good," said Profitt, sounding like that little boy again. "I've tried to make up for the bad with as much good as I can."

"Sometimes it's just not enough," said the priest. "Sometimes the sins far outweigh the good."

"But why take it out on the innocent?" asked Profitt. "Janet hadn't deserved what she got."

"She sold her soul for money. She entered in a loveless relationship for money."

Profitt looked at the priest and tried to figure out what was happening. There was no comfort in his words. They were stinging, biting words that filled Profitt with anger and hate and overwhelming sorrow.

"The chickens have come home to roost," said the priest as his features seemed to change in front of Profitt's eyes. And suddenly Profitt understood exactly what the priest had been talking about and knew that it was time for him to pay his debt to his friends.

22 | Chameleon

Obo sat at the computer, typing with a speed that was amazing. It looked as if he were robotic, his fingers computer-driven. He sat with his eyes closed, opening them only to look at the next page of the report. He could take it all in with a quick glance and then put it all into the computer in seconds.

Brackett stood where Obo normally did, looking out the window. He couldn't understand why the view fascinated Obo. All he could see was a small section of the street and the roof of a building a couple of floors lower. Almost nothing of interest.

Daily was sitting in a chair, her feet up on the table, staring up, at the ceiling. "When an investigation is stalled," she said, "you begin again. Look at the evidence, talk to the witnesses, and see if there isn't something that was missed on the first go-around."

"We're not exactly stalled," said Brackett.

"Come on, Loot," said Daily. "What have you got on your mind? What are you going to do?"

"Shift through the stuff we found a little more thoroughly."

Daily laughed. "I was thinking about the Profitt case. It seems that the two are related."

"I'd have to agree," said Brackett.

"Then we go talk to Profitt again. He has to know something that he hasn't told us. Might give us a clue."

Brackett turned from the window. "You about done with that, Obo?"

"Yes, Loot. Almost all done."

"Let's see what we get from the mainframe," said Brackett. "Then we can do something."

"You're the boss."

Father Robert was gone, having changed in front of Profitt's eyes. His features had seemed to slither away, dissolving as if sprayed with a heavy acid. His scalp crawled and hair sprouted and grew and curled.

"What . . . ?" said Profitt, his voice low, filled with awe, surprise, and terror. "What?"

Hanssen's body changed, becoming thinner, younger, and suddenly he was gone, replaced by another man. A young man who was grinning broadly.

Profitt had stood and backed away from the horror going on in front of him. He had lifted a hand, as if to shield his eyes, but then didn't want to block his view. He pushed himself into the corner, trying to get farther away, but the wall stopped him.

"I," he started to say. And then, suddenly, "Jason!"

"Oh, you remember," said Jason Argon, sitting on the couch where the priest had been. "I thought you'd have forgotten me by now." He waved a hand. "A man with all this could easily forget the friend he left to die."

"No!" said Profitt, his voice high and tight and unnatural. "You're dead."

"Nope," said Argon, his tone conversational. "I'm alive and well, no thanks to you."

"That thing . . . animal . . . dragged you off. Killed you."

"Ah," said Argon. "Is that the story?"

Profitt sank to the floor. It felt as if his knees had melted and his muscles no longer worked. "How?"

"Yes," said Argon happily, "that is the question, isn't it? How?"

"I saw . . ."

"What you saw," said Argon, his voice hardening, "was the opportunity to dump me and keep everything for yourself. You saw an opportunity and you took it, regardless of the circumstances."

"There was nothing I could do," said Profitt.

"Nothing," said Argon. "You didn't try. You let that . . . that thing drag me away and didn't do a damned thing to stop it."

It suddenly dawned on Profitt that he was talking to a friend who had died more than twenty years earlier. He hadn't aged a day. He hadn't changed a bit. Except that he had walked in as . . . Father Robert.

"I . . ."

"Yeah," snapped Argon. "You. It was always you. Never me or Kincaid. Always you. And when the chips were down, you did nothing to help me. Now you live here, surrounded by luxury, never thinking about what you let happen out there."

Profitt could no longer speak. He could only stare at the man who looked just like the man who had died so many years earlier.

"So many plans," said Argon. "So many plans. Thoresson was supposed to help me. I was going to bring down your empire. I was going to destroy your personal life." He stopped and shook his head. "Loyalty is a strange thing." He chuckled to himself. "Thoresson quit. But who cares."

Profitt didn't react to the news. He sat staring at Argon, stunned by the sudden appearance of the man he'd thought dead for over twenty years.

Argon took a deep breath. "The creature didn't kill me. Or maybe it did. I've never been able to figure that part of it out. I'm still me. I have my memories, my thoughts, but I've been . . . what? I've been trained? Inspired? Absorbed? I don't really know. But now I'm stronger and better and smarter than I was. I can feel the presence in the back of my mind giving instructions to me."

Argon turned and looked down at Profitt. "You've become a child who just learned that the monsters under the bed exist. That the beast in the closet will come out at night to kill and eat you."

He laughed out loud. "Revenge is so sweet, especially when

the victim realizes there is nothing he can do about it. He has to realize why it is happening or it's no good. I know that now. I didn't understand it before."

Profitt didn't move.

"That damned assassin," said Argon, shaking his head. "All he had to do was come in here and kill your wife. Quick. Simple. But your Bodyguard robot detected him and disposed of him. I must admit that I was a little surprised and a little in awe of that robot. Too bad the police impounded it. Too bad that O'Shaughnessy was so inept."

"Why are you doing this?"

"Because you deserve it, you dummy."

"But I didn't do anything," said Profitt.

"Exactly!" yelled Argon. "You did nothing!" He slammed his fist down on the arm of the chair. "I was dragged into the bush. Dragged into the jungle and you stood your ground and watched! *You did nothing!"*

"There was nothing I could do."

"No! You could have tried to help me. You could have followed. We had weapons, but you didn't go for them. You didn't try to get help. That creature dragged me into its . . . its lair and broke my legs so that I couldn't get away. Snapped them and left me screaming in the pain until I passed out. While you stayed safe and warm on the ship."

Profitt didn't speak. He sat with his head bowed, tears streaming down his face.

"I lay in that cave for days and listened to the dripping of water that I couldn't get to, praying that you or Kincaid would find me. I prayed as that beast entered and chewed on my living flesh, sucking the life out of me." His voice dropped to a whisper. "But you never came. You left me there to live or die."

"We were sick. Kincaid died. I was lucky to survive," said Profitt.

"Sure. Lucky. You were lucky. Funny how that worked, isn't it," said Argon.

Profitt shook his head. "I tried . . ."

"Sure." Argon stood up and walked to the windows, looking

out. "It's sure beautiful here. I'm going to enjoy owning all this."

He turned and said, "You always were a coward. I knew that from the first moment we took off into space that you were a coward." He sat down behind the desk and reached out, touching the pens, the blotter, the lamp. Rubbing his hands over the things as if to prove that they were real. "This is nice. Very nice."

Glancing at Profitt, he said, "All this wouldn't have been necessary. If the police had done their job . . . but then, you and I wouldn't have had the chance to meet this way."

He grinned at Profitt. "Oh, yeah, I'm responsible for the death of your wife. I did it. I killed her myself because O'Shaughnessy screwed that up. I killed her and tried to make you look guilty but that damned locked door . . . hadn't thought of that. I keep having to revise the plan. Nothing seems to work right for me."

"How?"

"Oh, don't be stupid," snapped Argon. "I came in here as a priest . . ."

"But Klaus wasn't . . ."

"Not Klaus. I can do anything I want. Think of an object and change to become that object. Nobody notices an extra chair or table. Waited for you to break in and find the body. I was sure the police would arrest you because there would be no one else to arrest."

"What are you?"

"No!" said Argon. "First you're going to listen to me. First you're going to hear about those days in the cave with the broken legs, praying for help and then praying to die and finally dying, after a fashion, only to become conscious again, but looking down at my body. I had been absorbed. Changed into something else. I was no longer me.

"That's quite a trip," said Argon. "First you're dead and then you're not and then you discover that you can be anything that you want to be. Visualize it hard enough and your body changes into that person or that thing. No pain. No hurt. Just a quiet re-forming of the body's structure."

Profitt suddenly stood up. He wiped at the sweat beaded on his face. Wiped the tears from his cheeks. He stared at Argon, sudden defiance in his eyes. "You can't hold me here. You don't have the strength. Didn't have it when we were partners and you don't have it now."

"You just don't get the picture, do you?" said Argon conversationally. "I am more than I was. I am stronger and smarter and more alive."

"No," said Profitt. "You're weak. Only the weak search for revenge. Only the weak die in the jungle rather than survive. And you have no weapon. I'm walking out of here and getting the police."

"And have them look for whom? Father Robert? Jason Argon. Maybe your private secretary . . ."

But Profitt was no longer interested in listening. He screamed, and rushed forward, his hands out so that he could grab Argon by the throat and strangle him. Break his neck and then dispose of the body.

Before he'd taken a step, Argon was gone. There was a shimmering, and a beast appeared, striped like a tiger, claws like the largest bear that had ever lived on any planet, and a snout filled with large pointed teeth. The hide looked tough, and the limbs were as thick as tree trunks. It was a creature that would take a laser blast and not even feel it. It snarled once, saliva dripping from its mouth; its eyes, smoldering like day-old coals, glowed. The stench from the beast filled the office.

Profitt felt the strength drain from his body. His knees were weak and he collapsed to the carpeted floor. He put his hands over his eyes, knowing that the creature could take off his head with a single swipe of one of its gigantic paws.

Then, suddenly, Argon was back, his voice soft. "There is nothing you can do now."

Profitt looked up and saw the young man had returned. He hesitated and then asked, "Why Janet?"

"Because she was yours. Because she was there. Because

you deserved it. Because it made me feel better, taking some-thing away from you."

"And Linda?"

"Because the police seemed to believe you innocent. So that the police would take a longer look at you. So that you would spend the remainder of your days in jail thinking about what you'd done. Because she had betrayed me in the end. But it's too late for that now."

"I'll give you half. Acknowledge your role in the discovery. You'll be seen as a hero, returning from the dead after so many years." Profitt was talking faster now, realizing that he had little time left unless he could convince Argon.

"You don't get it, do you?" said Argon. "I don't need half of what you have because I can have everything."

"It wasn't my fault," said Profitt, his voice higher. "We looked for you but then we got sick. Both of us and we both fig-ured that you were dead. There was nothing we could do."

"And there is nothing that you can do now."

Profitt stared at Argon for a moment. "We were friends once."

"We were never friends," said Argon. "And any feelings that I had about you died with me so long ago. Now it is time for me to get even."

"The police are on the way," said Profitt desperately.

"I don't care."

"Haven't you already done enough to me?" asked Profitt. "You've turned my life upside down."

Argon laughed again. "Done enough to you? No. There is more to be done to you . . ."

"My secretary is right outside that door."

"Soundproofed walls and doors," said Argon. "You like your privacy and you like the silence. You're a dead man."

"No!" wailed Profitt. He scrambled to his feet and screamed again, *"No!"*

Argon advanced on him, grinning evilly. "Scream all you want. That just makes it better for me."

23 | In the Entire History of Motion Pictures, the Cavalry Has Never Failed to Arrive in the Nick of Time

Daily drove this time because Brackett didn't want to. He wanted to ride along and look out the window and survey the city. Get a feel for it because it was becoming clearer that they would be on the planet for a while. With no leads and no evidence, there wasn't much that they could do.

"You think that Profitt did it himself, Loot?"

Brackett looked at her, studying her profile as she watched the traffic swirling around them. "Nah. Motive just doesn't seem to be there. No reason for him to do his wife. He cuts her loose and she gets a little dough. But there isn't anything that suggests he wanted to cut her loose."

"Then it's an outsider."

"Obviously. I would have put my money on one of the women working for him. Eliminate the competition. But it's not the way women operate, not to mention the fact there is no evidence to support it."

"Yeah," agreed Daily. "I can see one of them killing Janet to get her out of the way, but it would have to be someone with a real shot at getting the boss. None of it works. Besides, we've got that damned locked room."

"Which puts the finger back on Profitt. There must be a secret way out of there and he'd be the only one to know it. Case is strange."

They slowed and turned a corner. Profitt's building loomed

over them. Brackett pointed at the curb in front of it and said, "Pull in there."

"Sure thing." She guided the hover car to the curb and then stopped. It settled to the ground and the hum of the engine died quickly.

Brackett opened his door and climbed out, into the stifling heat of the early afternoon. He shielded his eyes with his hand as he looked up, at the penthouse, lost in a low-hanging cloud. That gave the building an unreal look. Like something that actually reached up into heaven.

They entered the hotel and walked across the floor to the bank of elevators. Brackett waved at the clerk on duty, telling her that they didn't need help. She nodded in response and went back to her work. Before they got in the main elevators, Brackett said, "He'll probably be in the office now."

"Right."

They walked around the corner, to the private elevators, and entered one. They took it up, and then exited, into the wide corridor/waiting room outside the main office complex. When they reached the closed double doors, Brackett touched the bell and held up his badge for the button camera.

There was no response until the doors opened and Rachel stood there, holding the knobs of both doors as she leaned forward. "Can I help you?"

"We're here to see your boss."

"I'm afraid that he is busy at the moment. Father Robert is with him. If you'll have a seat, I'll let him know that you're here."

"No," said Brackett, "I don't believe we'll wait this time. We'll just go on in."

Rachel held her ground until Brackett stood nose to nose with her, and then she retreated, leaving the doors wide open. She spun and hurried to her desk, bent over toward the intercom, and announced, "The police are here."

Before Profitt could respond, Brackett was at the door to the office. He grabbed the doorknob and twisted. It was locked. Brackett turned toward Rachel.

"I don't have the key."

"If it's not opened in ten seconds, I'm going to break it down."

He felt the knob twist in his hand and the door was pulled open. Profitt stood in front of him, looking a little pale. Sweat was beaded on his forehead.

"What do you want?"

"I have a few questions for you," said Brackett. "Mind if I come in?"

"I have business to conduct," said Profitt.

Rachel turned and said, "I told them you were busy. I told them that Father Robert was with you."

"Father Robert has left," said Profitt.

"Then there is no reason not to answer the questions," said Brackett.

"Oh, all right," snapped Profitt. "What is it?"

"Not here," said Brackett, stepping forward. "In your office."

Profitt didn't move. Brackett stopped a foot away and waited. Again the tactic worked. Profitt moved back, out of the way.

Brackett, and then Daily, entered the office. Profitt turned and walked to his desk. He sat down behind it and watched the two Star Cops. "Now, what is so important that you have to burst in here?"

"Mr. Profitt," said Brackett evenly, "you invited us here originally. In fact, demanded that we come here. Now it seems that you no longer desire our assistance."

"Lieutenant," said Profitt, "you have done nothing to solve the crimes committed here. You have bungled every aspect of the investigation and I fully intend to report this latest intrusion to your superiors."

"What happened to the spirit of cooperation that you displayed just a few hours ago?" asked Brackett.

"It died with your bungling. Now, let's get on with it."

Brackett moved to the closest visitor's chair and sat down. He glanced back at Daily. As she moved forward, she stopped suddenly and then pointed.

"What the hell?"

Brackett leaned to the right and sticking out, barely visible, was the toe of a shoe. "What . . . ?"

Suddenly Profitt was on his feet, moving. Brackett kicked his chair over and struggled with his coat, trying to draw his weapon. Daily had hers out and pointed but didn't fire it.

"You are under arrest," she announced in a loud voice.

Brackett rolled to his left and pulled his own weapon, ripping the cloth as he did so. He was up on one knee. "We have you covered, Profitt."

Before their eyes, Profitt began to change. His shoulders expanded and his arms lengthened. Razor-sharp claws appeared on his fingers. He swiped at Daily suddenly, and as she jumped to the side, the claws ripped at her shoulder, tearing her blouse and drawing blood.

Brackett fired then, the beam stabbing out, touching the thing on the chest. It roared in fury and its hide changed subtly so that it reflected the beam. A hole appeared in the wall behind Brackett.

The beast advanced, reaching out to kill Brackett. Daily fired, and the flesh around its ear began to pop and sizzle, sounding like a steak over hot coals. It roared in pain and whirled, now swinging at Daily. She ducked under the huge arm and danced away, holding down the trigger of her weapon.

"Hit the eyes," yelled Brackett. "Hit it in the eyes." He fired at the head, but missed. The beam burned the wall, setting part of it on fire. Smoke began to fill the office.

Rachel appeared in the door, saw the beast, and screamed. She ducked back out of the way but continued screaming.

Daily, blood staining the sleeve of her blouse, aimed again. She held the weapon in both hands, trying to steady it. She hit the creature in the face, slicing away a bit of flesh. Blood exploded from it, splashing the desk, but that didn't seem to slow the creature.

Brackett had backed away until he was up against the wall. He pointed his weapon, but didn't fire. He watched as the hide shimmered, changing until it was all highly reflective, making it difficult to use the laser. Brackett calculated the shot, aimed, and pulled the trigger. The beam bounced off and cut into the ceiling. Flames spread along the material, but Brackett held his aim steady, trying to burn through to the brain, as he tried not to kill Daily.

Suddenly the creature roared and threw itself across the desk, its claws held out like a dozen razor-sharp daggers. It kicked over a chair and then dropped. Brackett waited until the last instant and then dived to the right, rolling. He whirled, firing again.

Daily was standing near the door, her weapon aimed at the creature. She fired. The beam bounced around like it was hitting a mirrored ball. It destroyed the light fixtures above them.

Brackett leapt to the back of it suddenly, hugging it. He pressed his pistol against its side and pulled the trigger. He felt the weapon grow hot as the beams reflected around, but he didn't let up. He prayed that he could burn through the hide before the pistol exploded in his hand.

Now that she couldn't shoot at it, Daily leapt forward. She screamed, trying to draw its attention to her. She waved her arms at it, willing it to turn toward her. Again it tried to rake her with its claws, but she was too far away.

The shape changed suddenly and Brackett lost his grip. He fell to the floor and tried to roll, but he was up against the desk now. He flipped to his back and fired his weapon at the belly of the creature as it turned toward him.

The hide was no longer reflective. It shimmered and changed, until it was a dull, muddy brown. It fell to its knees and held up a hand to ward off the laser.

Daily, still on her feet, pointed the weapon at the beast's head, but held her fire.

Brackett was afraid of it. He didn't know what it could do, how fast it could heal itself. He burned through its belly. Blood poured from the wound, pooling on the floor. The flesh seemed to bubble and then boil. The creature fell to the floor. Its shape changed rapidly until it was just a twenty-year-old human lying on the carpet, blood covering its chest. There was a hole in the belly and part of the skull was missing so that the brain showed through.

Brackett released the trigger and then climbed to his feet. He steadied himself against the desk, his eyes on the dead man in front of him.

"What in the hell was that?" asked Daily.

"I don't know." He glanced at her, saw the blood. "You okay?"

"I'm fine."

Brackett nodded and said, "Check the other one." He refused to look away, afraid that the dead creature was playing a trick on him.

Daily moved over and rolled the body to its back, fully expecting to see that it was Father Robert. She almost fell back as she recognized it. She stared down at the face, almost unable to believe her eyes.

"Hey, it's Profitt."

"Yeah," said Brackett. "I thought it might be."

"But that was Profitt."

"No," said Brackett, still studying the creature. "That was a lot of things, but it wasn't Profitt."

24 | Case Closed

Hughes sat at the table, his hands folded, looking at Brackett, Daily, and Obo. "How did you know that it was the priest?"

Brackett was quiet for a moment and then said, "I could lie to you and tell you that we'd tracked the whole thing, but that wouldn't be true. We were following the trail of the assassin and walked in at the right time. We lucked into it by being in the right place."

"Let me get this straight," said Hughes. "The priest, Ambassador Gleason, and this old pal of Profitt were all the same person?"

"And Lana Diamond," said Brackett. "And who knows how many others?"

Daily spoke up. "There have been stories of shape shifters on several planets. Most of them are primitive creatures that are able to change their shape enough to blend in with the rocky bottom of a stream, or to hide in the branches of a tree or a bush or the like. This is the first complex creature that we have run into."

"But Argon was a human," said Hughes.

"That's where we get into trouble," said Brackett. "He started as a human, but was altered so that he became a shape shifter."

"That would mean," said Hughes slowly, "that it happened on this planet."

"It's going to make your investigations interesting from now on," said Brackett.

"What do you mean?"

"If there was one, why not two, or three, or a hundred?" asked Brackett.

Hughes was quiet. "We've explored this planet. Mapping with the latest equipment. Searches for indigenous life forms. Zoological research to discover and classify all the animal life . . ."

"A shape shifter can blend in with the environment so that it won't be discovered. Besides, this breed seems to have intelligence."

"Then we can't tell who might be one and who isn't," said Hughes.

"Which explains how OBrien and Ryan lost Gleason. They didn't recognize him when he left the church. They thought it was the priest," said Brackett.

Hughes shook his head slowly. "I don't see how we're going to . . ."

"Look at the bright side," said Brackett. "Humans have been on this planet for a long time and this is the first time you've run into one of them. That probably means that they're a rare species."

"How do we know?" asked Hughes. "How do we know that it's the first time?"

"That is the problem, isn't it?" said Brackett.

Brackett hadn't thought that the 107th could look so good, but the moment he stepped off the shuttle, he knew that he was happy to be back. He was away from the blinding sun, the heat and humidity, and the people. Away from the case below, coming back to the precinct with a solution, though he and Daily had stumbled over the solution.

Outside the shuttle bay, Brackett stopped long enough to inhale a lungful of the metallic-smelling, recycled air of the precinct. He then looked at both Daily and Obo and said, "Now that smells like air."

"Captain Carnes isn't going to like our handing the collar over to the locals," said Daily.

"Hell, they deserved it. Hughes was on the right track. We just blundered in at the most opportune moment. Though it does prove the value of following the procedures. Had we not been doing that, we'd never have gotten the answer. Besides, we solved the crime we were sent to solve. We look good and we've made a few friends on the planet."

"Still . . ."

Brackett laughed. "You can't get under my skin with talk of Carnes. I'm too happy at being home."

"Obo buy the first round."

"Okay, Obo," said Brackett. "And I've got the second." He looked pointedly at Daily.

"Well, hell, I've got the third," she said. "Though I don't know why you want to drink."

"Because it's time," said Brackett.

"Can we at least take the time to drop our gear in our cabins?" asked Daily.

"If you don't take too long," said Brackett.

Carnes appeared at the end of the corridor, walking fast. As he approached, he said, "I'll expect a full report, on my desk, by zero eight hundred tomorrow."

"I can give you a verbal report now," said Brackett.

"No, Lieutenant. I want it in writing, suitable for input to the mainframe."

"Captain," said Brackett, "we just arrived."

"I'm aware of that fact, but we all have work to do. Now, you have your orders."

Daily spoke up. "Yes, sir."

As Carnes disappeared, Brackett said, "That was nice of the old boy. Show up to welcome us back."

An instant later Tate was running down the corridor, holding a hand in the air and shouting like a commuter who was trying to stop the bus.

"Now what?" said Daily, slightly disgusted.

Tate slid to a halt and said, "You promised that I would be in on the kill."

"I'm not sure that we promised that," said Brackett evenly.

"I was supposed to get the story if I held off on reporting the earlier news."

"Well," said Brackett, "what do you want to know?"

Tate was taken aback momentarily. He stood, looking from Brackett to Daily to Obo and then back again. Finally he said, "Everything."

"That'll take quite a while and we have plans. In fact, have orders. We have to prepare our reports for the captain," said Brackett.

"I did you a favor by keeping quiet," said Tate.

Brackett looked at his fellow officers. "You think we should help this young man?"

"Why not?" said Daily.

"Yes," added Obo.

"Okay," said Brackett. "Local newsies and their friends got the preliminary story. Profitt, his wife, and a secretary are dead. Some are saying that it was a love triangle that went wrong. That's not it. We'll give it all to you. Tomorrow."

"Somebody is going to get there first."

"Nope," said Brackett. "We've got the story locked down. You can have it tomorrow."

Tate realized that he couldn't push it. If he did, they'd tell him nothing. He'd have to be patient. "Tomorrow," he said. "First thing."

"The Cup and Hole at nine tomorrow."

"I'll be there." Tate hesitated, as if there was more that he wanted to say. He realized that none of the officers was going to talk to him. "Well, I guess I'll get going."

As Tate walked back down the corridor, Brackett said, "There goes a young man who's going to burn himself out."

"We do not drink now?" asked Obo.

"Hell, yes," said Brackett. "What's he going to do? Fire us? After all we've solved our case in short order."

"And after we have the drinks," said Daily, "we'll put together the report."

Brackett shot her a glance. "We could work all night on it," he said.

"In my cabin?" asked Daily.

"Obo need to get his sleep."

"I would think, Obo," said Brackett, "that you could put together your report, detailing the various stages of the investigation as you conducted them, on your own, as a supplement to the main investigative report."

"Yes," agreed Obo.

"Then it's settled," said Brackett. "First a drink to unwind, and then to the reports."

"If you insist," said Daily.

"I do."